# Elenora Mandragora

## Daughter of Merlin

THANK YOU TO CHARLOTTE AND THE ENTIRE TEAM
FOR THEIR TRUST AND SUPPORT.

FOR OUR LITTLE APOLLINE.

*Séverine and Thomas*

Become our fan on Facebook **facebook.com/idwpublishing**
Follow us on Twitter **@idwpublishing**
Subscribe to us on YouTube **youtube.com/idwpublishing**
See what's new on Tumblr **tumblr.idwpublishing.com**
Check us out on Instagram **instagram.com/idwpublishing**

ISBN: 978-1-68405-008-6                    20 19 18 17  1 2 3 4

COVER BY
THOMAS LABOUROT

TRANSLATION BY
EDWARD GAUVIN

EDITED BY
JUSTIN EISINGER
AND ALONZO SIMON

PRODUCTION BY
RON ESTEVEZ

PUBLISHER
TED ADAMS

ELENORA MANDRAGORA: DAUGHTER OF MERLIN. NOVEMBER 2017. FIRST
PRINTING. © 2017 Rue de Sèvres, Paris. Translation © 2017 Idea and Design
Works, LLC. The IDW logo is registered in the U.S. Patent and Trademark Office.
IDW Publishing, a division of Idea and Design Works, LLC. Editorial offices: 2765
Truxtun Road, San Diego, CA 92106. Any similarities to persons living or dead are
purely coincidental. With the exception of artwork used for review purposes,
none of the contents of this publication may be reprinted without the permission
of Idea and Design Works, LLC. Printed in Korea.
IDW Publishing does not read or accept unsolicited submissions of ideas, stories,
or artwork.

Ted Adams, CEO & Publisher
Greg Goldstein, President & COO
Robbie Robbins, EVP/Sr. Graphic Artist
Chris Ryall, Chief Creative Officer
David Hedgecock, Editor-in-Chief
Laurie Windrow, Senior VP of Sales & Marketing
Matthew Ruzicka, CPA, Chief Financial Officer
Lorelei Bunjes, VP of Digital Services
Jerry Bennington, VP of New Product Development

First published in France as *Aliénor Mandragore - Merlin est mort, vive Merlin !*
© 2015 Rue de Sèvres, Paris

# Elenora Mandragora

## Daughter of Merlin

STORY
**Séverine Gauthier**

ART
**Thomas Labourot**

COLORS
**Grelin & Thomas Labourot**

LETTERING
**Ron Estevez**

# THE PEOPLE
## of the Forest

## MERLIN, Wizard

Merlin is a wizard, the greatest druid in the forest of Broceliande. Born of a human and a demon, he gets his amazing powers from the demonic side of his family. Merlin spends most of his time tending to his Mushroomery in a particularly dark, damp part of the woods where he's always dragging his daughter ELENORA for endless lessons. A real "papa hen," always fussing over his daughter, Merlin hopes to see ELENORA carry on the family tradition and, someday, become a legend in her own right.

## ELENORA, Daughter

ELENORA is Merlin's daughter. She lives with her father in the heart of the forest, where she takes lessons in druiding from him. Impish and undisciplined, ELENORA is a rather unremarkable student, and seems to have no talent for magic—that is, until the day her incredible gift manifests itself…

## MORGANA, Fairy

Morgana is Viviane's sister and Merlin's sworn enemy. They've been rivals forever, and never agree about anything except their cordial hatred of each other, always arguing about this, that, and the other thing. An accomplished magician and sorceress, Morgana also makes delicious honey in the hive where she lives among her protégés, the giant bees of Broceliande.

## VIVIANE, LA DAME DU LAC, Lady

Viviane lives in a crystal palace in the great Lake in the middle of Broceliande. She commands the creatures of the deep, and rarely leaves the chilly waters, with which she must remain in constant contact.

## LANCELOT DU LAC, Apprentice Knight

Apart from Viviane, who took him in, no one knows where the young Lancelot came from. Viviane instructs him in arts and letters, trying to instill in him the wisdom and courage he needs to become a true knight.

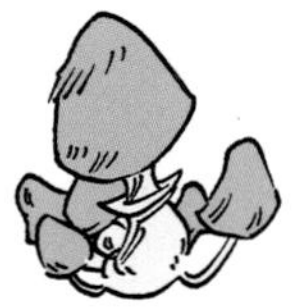

FOREST OF BROCELIANDE. THE MUSHROOMERY.

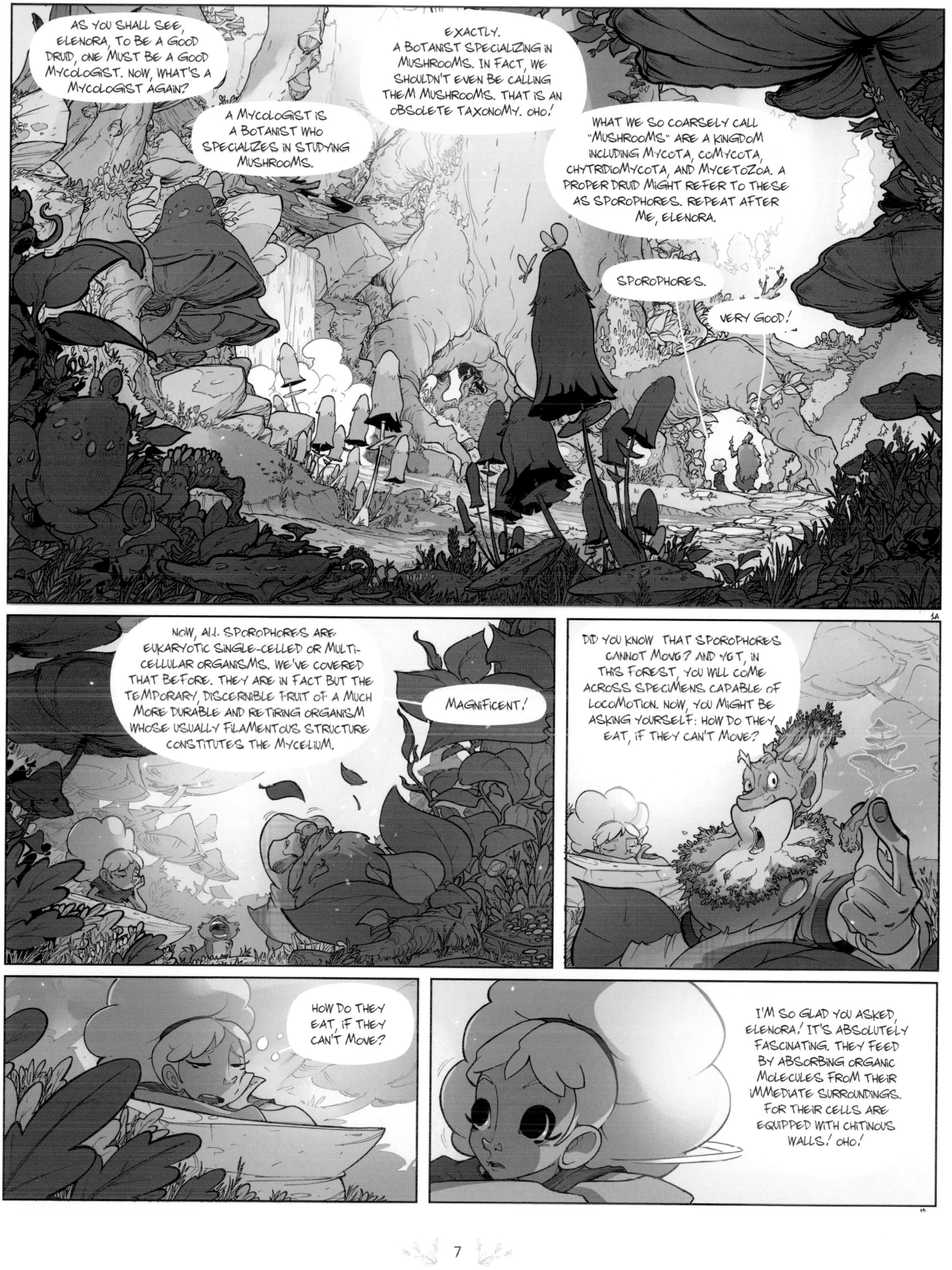
AS YOU SHALL SEE, ELENORA, TO BE A GOOD DRUID, ONE MUST BE A GOOD MYCOLOGIST. NOW, WHAT'S A MYCOLOGIST AGAIN?
A MYCOLOGIST IS A BOTANIST WHO SPECIALIZES IN STUDYING MUSHROOMS.
EXACTLY. A BOTANIST SPECIALIZING IN MUSHROOMS. IN FACT, WE SHOULDN'T EVEN BE CALLING THEM MUSHROOMS. THAT IS AN OBSOLETE TAXONOMY. OHO!
WHAT WE SO COARSELY CALL "MUSHROOMS" ARE A KINGDOM INCLUDING MYCOTA, COMYCOTA, CHYTRIDIOMYCOTA, AND MYCETOZOA. A PROPER DRUID MIGHT REFER TO THESE AS SPOROPHORES. REPEAT AFTER ME, ELENORA.
SPOROPHORES.
VERY GOOD!
NOW, ALL SPOROPHORES ARE EUKARYOTIC SINGLE-CELLED OR MULTI-CELLULAR ORGANISMS. WE'VE COVERED THAT BEFORE. THEY ARE IN FACT BUT THE TEMPORARY, DISCERNIBLE FRUIT OF A MUCH MORE DURABLE AND RETIRING ORGANISM WHOSE USUALLY FILAMENTOUS STRUCTURE CONSTITUTES THE MYCELIUM.
MAGNIFICENT!
DID YOU KNOW THAT SPOROPHORES CANNOT MOVE? AND YET, IN THIS FOREST, YOU WILL COME ACROSS SPECIMENS CAPABLE OF LOCOMOTION. NOW, YOU MIGHT BE ASKING YOURSELF: HOW DO THEY EAT, IF THEY CAN'T MOVE?
HOW DO THEY EAT, IF THEY CAN'T MOVE?
I'M SO GLAD YOU ASKED, ELENORA! IT'S ABSOLUTELY FASCINATING. THEY FEED BY ABSORBING ORGANIC MOLECULES FROM THEIR IMMEDIATE SURROUNDINGS. FOR THEIR CELLS ARE EQUIPPED WITH CHITINOUS WALLS! OHO!

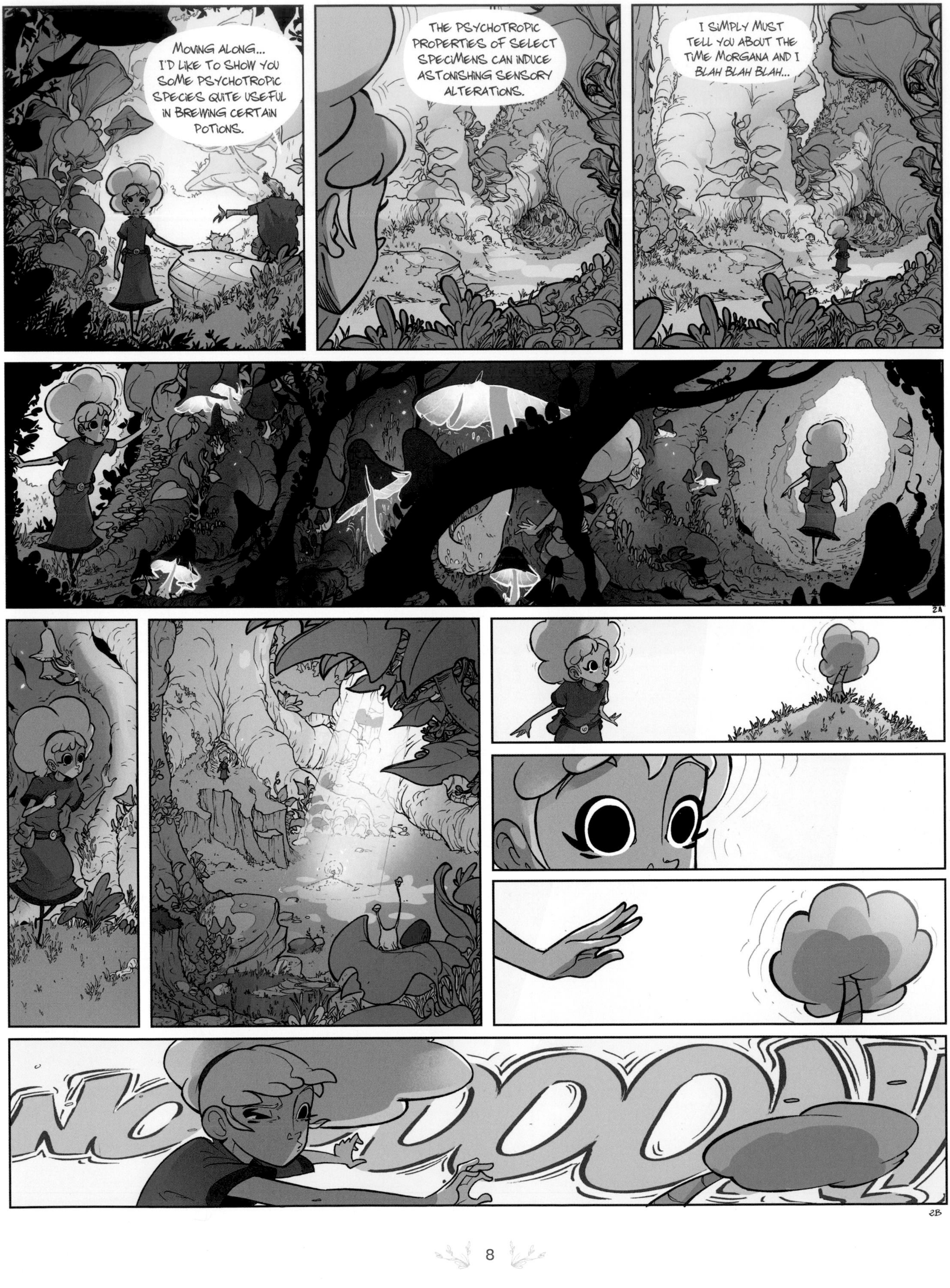
MOVING ALONG... I'D LIKE TO SHOW YOU SOME PSYCHOTROPIC SPECIES QUITE USEFUL IN BREWING CERTAIN POTIONS.
THE PSYCHOTROPIC PROPERTIES OF SELECT SPECIMENS CAN INDUCE ASTONISHING SENSORY ALTERATIONS.
I SIMPLY MUST TELL YOU ABOUT THE TIME MORGANA AND I BLAH BLAH BLAH...

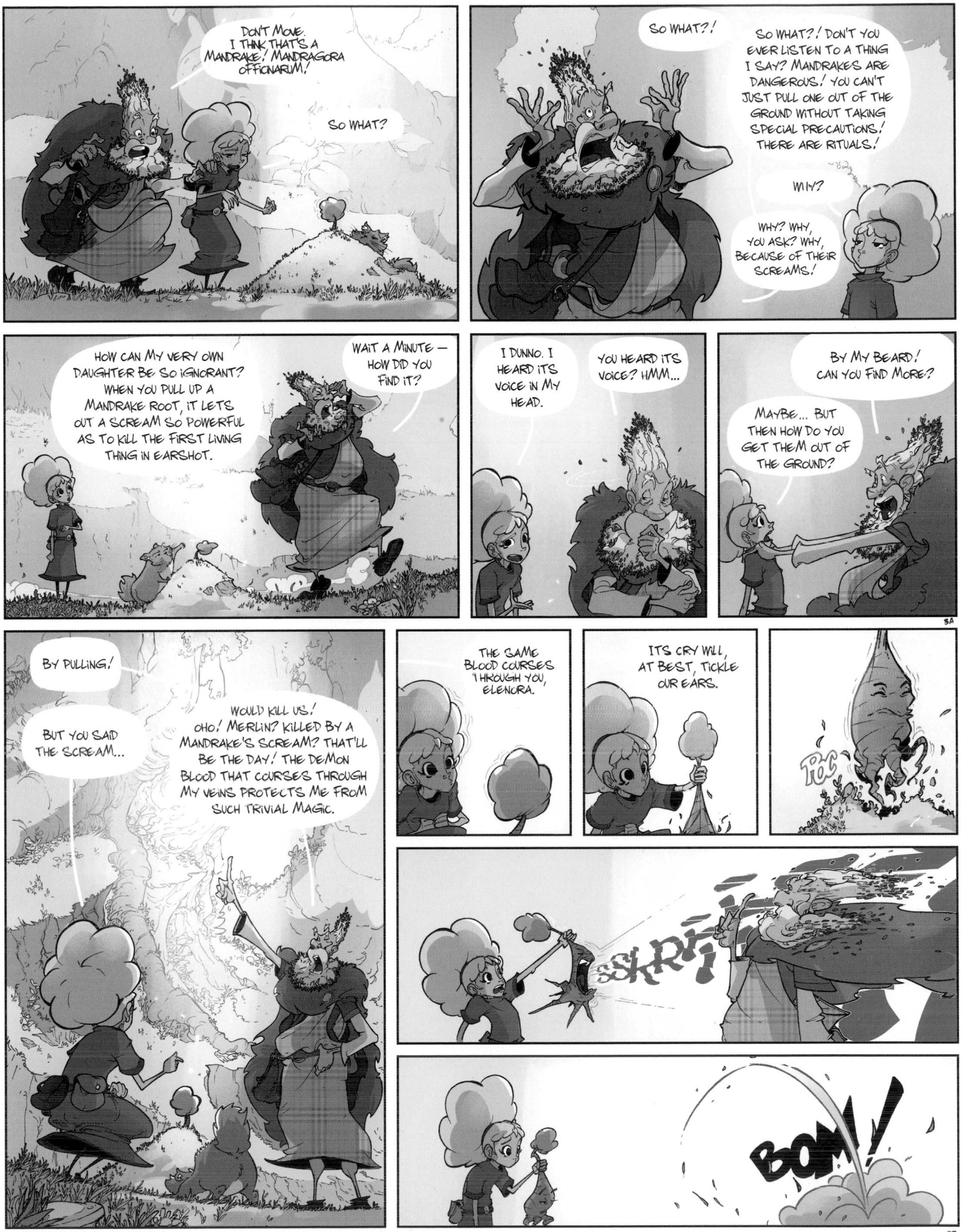
DON'T MOVE. I THINK THAT'S A MANDRAKE! MANDRAGORA OFFICINARUM!
SO WHAT?
SO WHAT?!
SO WHAT?! DON'T YOU EVER LISTEN TO A THING I SAY? MANDRAKES ARE DANGEROUS! YOU CAN'T JUST PULL ONE OUT OF THE GROUND WITHOUT TAKING SPECIAL PRECAUTIONS! THERE ARE RITUALS!
WHY?
WHY? WHY, YOU ASK? WHY, BECAUSE OF THEIR SCREAMS!
HOW CAN MY VERY OWN DAUGHTER BE SO IGNORANT? WHEN YOU PULL UP A MANDRAKE ROOT, IT LETS OUT A SCREAM SO POWERFUL AS TO KILL THE FIRST LIVING THING IN EARSHOT.
WAIT A MINUTE — HOW DID YOU FIND IT?
I DUNNO. I HEARD ITS VOICE IN MY HEAD.
YOU HEARD ITS VOICE? HMM...
BY MY BEARD! CAN YOU FIND MORE?
MAYBE... BUT THEN HOW DO YOU GET THEM OUT OF THE GROUND?
3A
BY PULLING!
BUT YOU SAID THE SCREAM...
WOULD KILL US! OHO! MERLIN? KILLED BY A MANDRAKE'S SCREAM? THAT'LL BE THE DAY! THE DEMON BLOOD THAT COURSES THROUGH MY VEINS PROTECTS ME FROM SUCH TRIVIAL MAGIC.
THE SAME BLOOD COURSES THROUGH YOU, ELENORA.
ITS CRY WILL, AT BEST, TICKLE OUR EARS.
POC
SSKRI
BOM!
3B

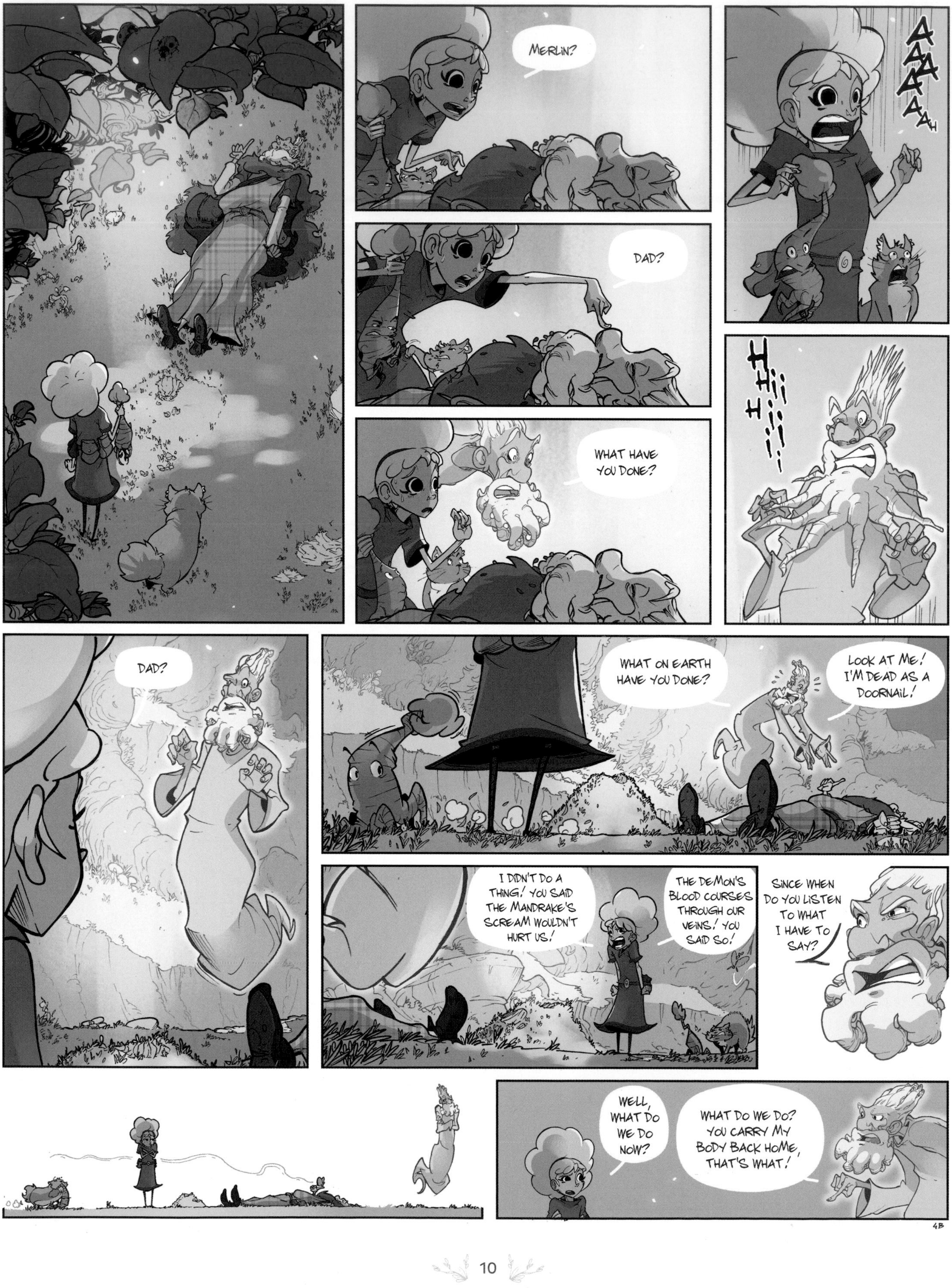
MERLIN?
AAAAAAH
DAD?
WHAT HAVE YOU DONE?
HHHiiiiiii
DAD?
WHAT ON EARTH HAVE YOU DONE?
LOOK AT ME! I'M DEAD AS A DOORNAIL!
I DIDN'T DO A THING! YOU SAID THE MANDRAKE'S SCREAM WOULDN'T HURT US!
THE DEMON'S BLOOD COURSES THROUGH OUR VEINS! YOU SAID SO!
SINCE WHEN DO YOU LISTEN TO WHAT I HAVE TO SAY?
WELL, WHAT DO WE DO NOW?
WHAT DO WE DO? YOU CARRY MY BODY BACK HOME, THAT'S WHAT!

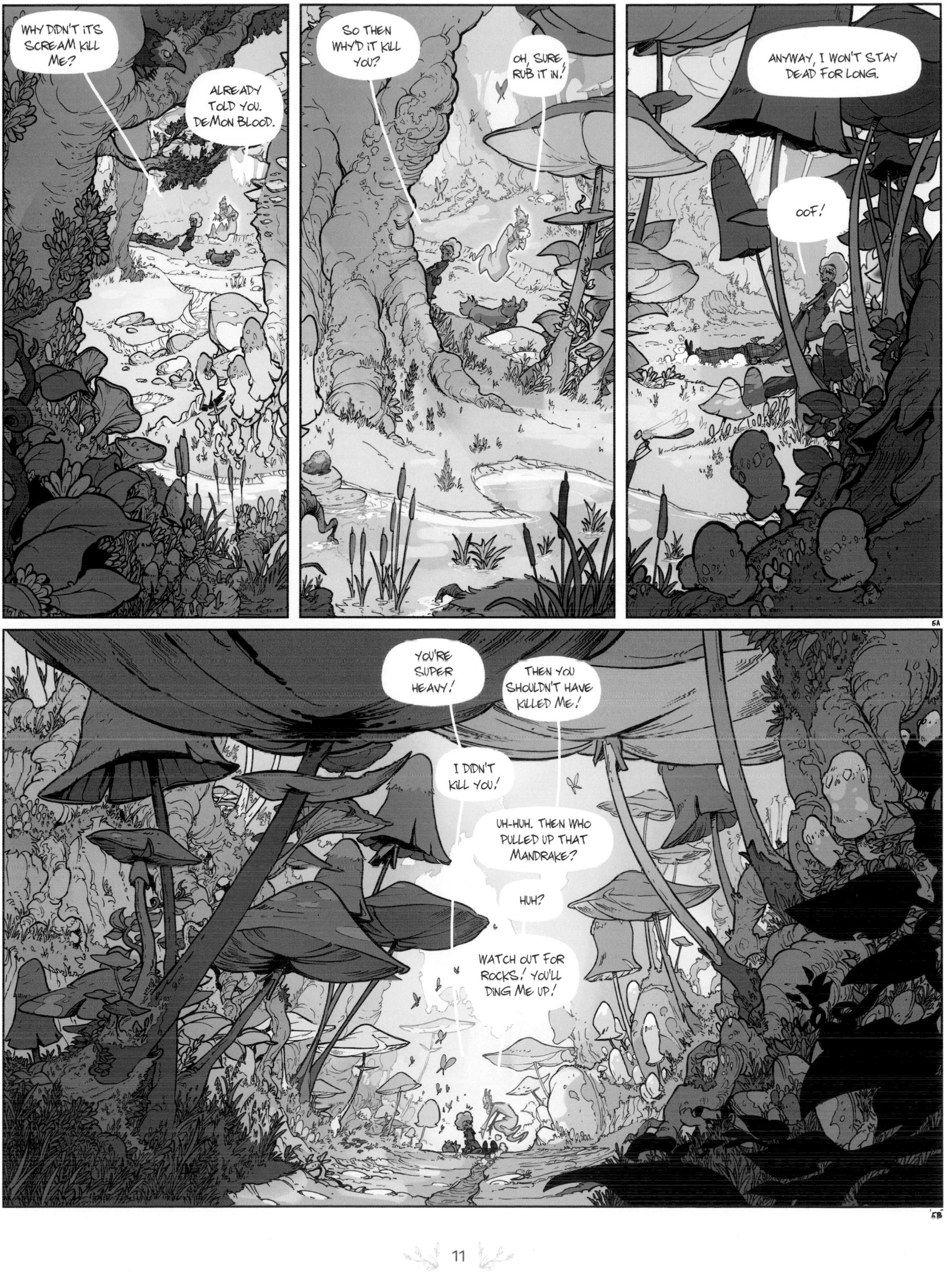
WHY DIDN'T ITS SCREAM KILL ME?
ALREADY TOLD YOU. DEMON BLOOD.
SO THEN WHY'D IT KILL YOU?
OH, SURE. RUB IT IN!
ANYWAY, I WON'T STAY DEAD FOR LONG.
OOF!
YOU'RE SUPER HEAVY!
THEN YOU SHOULDN'T HAVE KILLED ME!
I DIDN'T KILL YOU!
UH-HUH. THEN WHO PULLED UP THAT MANDRAKE?
HUH?
WATCH OUT FOR ROCKS! YOU'LL DING ME UP!

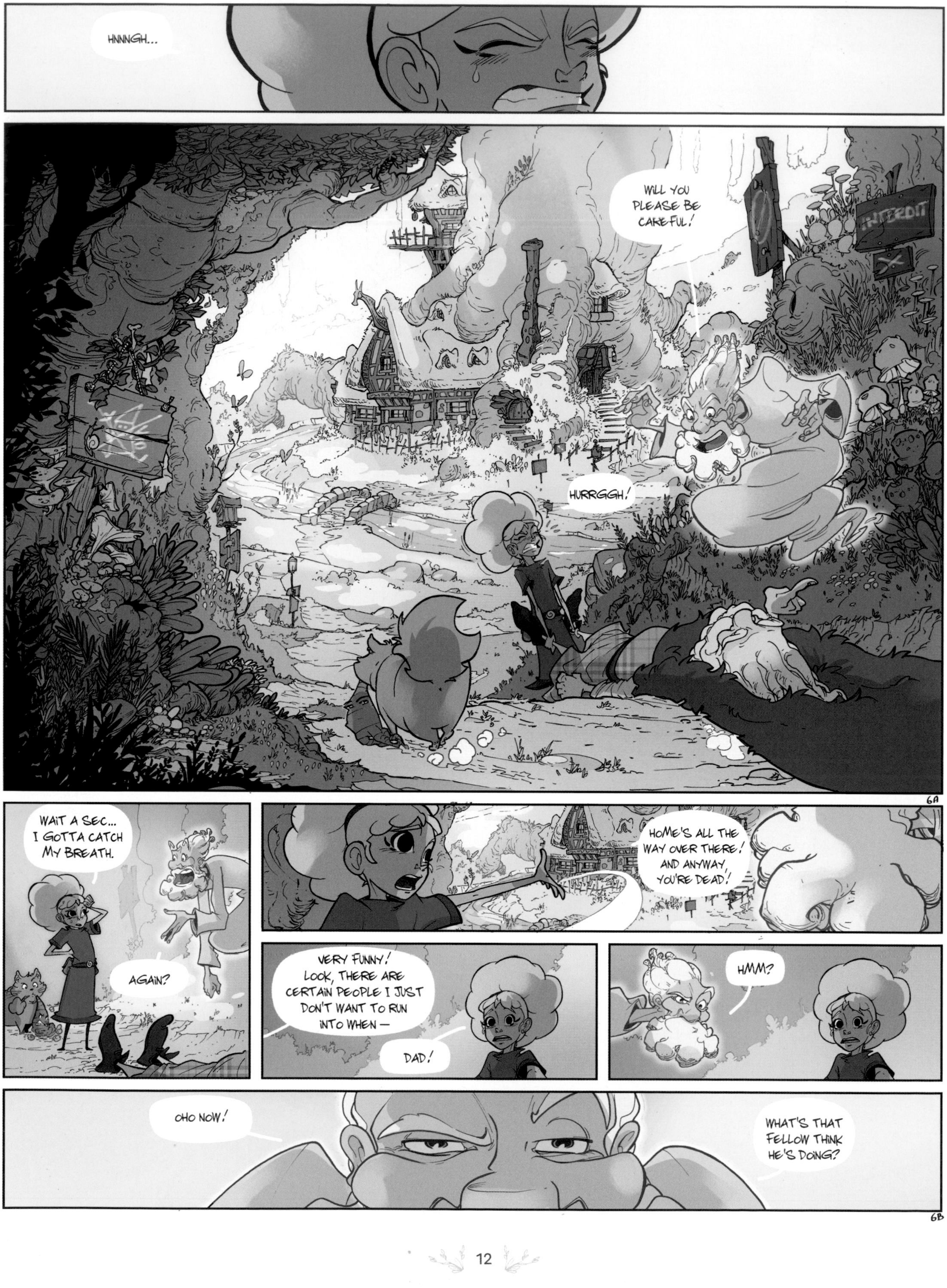

HNNNGH...
WILL YOU PLEASE BE CAREFUL!
INTERDIT
HURRGGH!
6A
WAIT A SEC... I GOTTA CATCH MY BREATH.
AGAIN?
HOME'S ALL THE WAY OVER THERE! AND ANYWAY, YOU'RE DEAD!
VERY FUNNY! LOOK, THERE ARE CERTAIN PEOPLE I JUST DON'T WANT TO RUN INTO WHEN —
DAD!
HMM?
OHO NOW!
WHAT'S THAT FELLOW THINK HE'S DOING?
6B

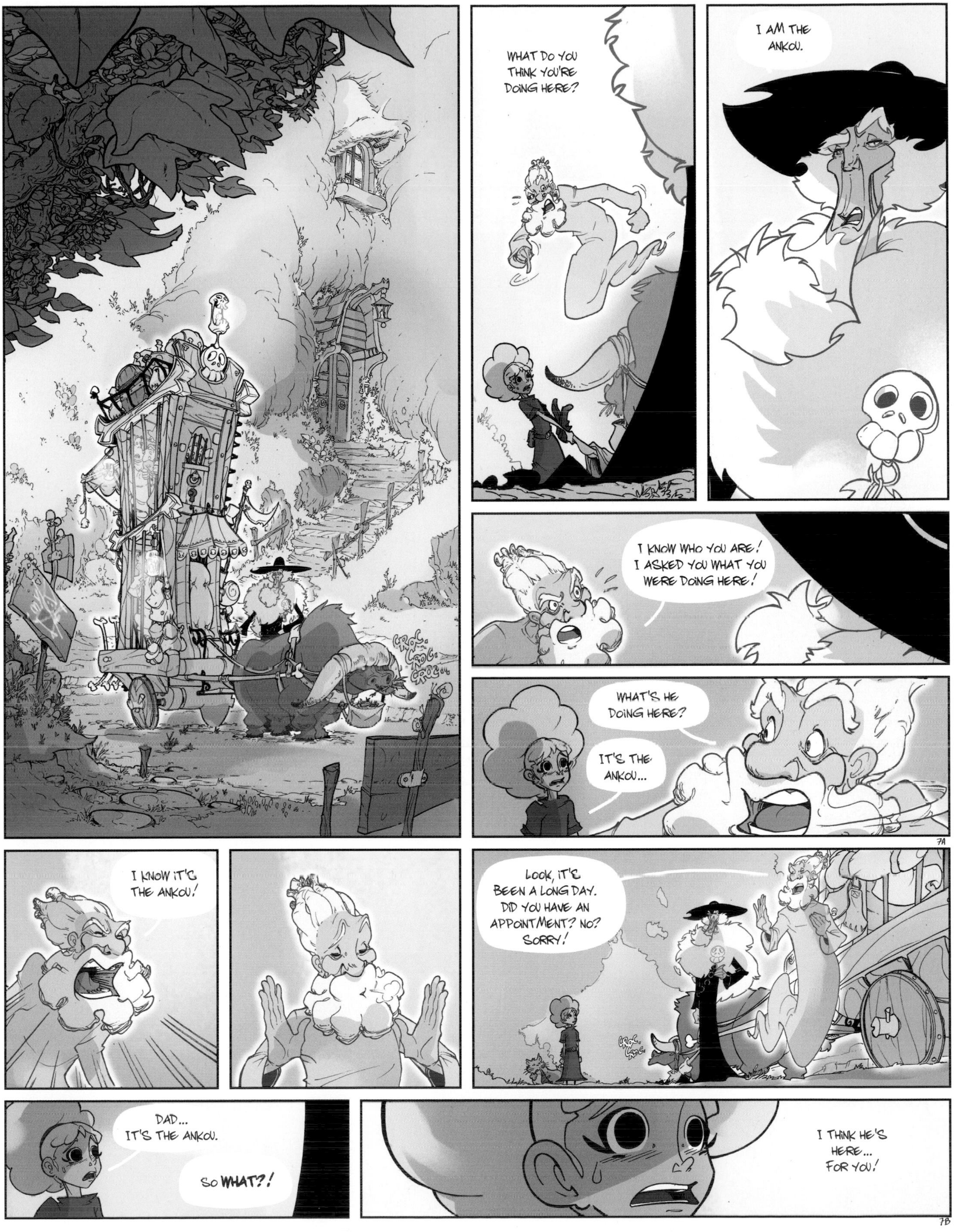
CROC CROC CROC
WHAT DO YOU THINK YOU'RE DOING HERE?
I AM THE ANKOU.
I KNOW WHO YOU ARE! I ASKED YOU WHAT YOU WERE DOING HERE!
WHAT'S HE DOING HERE?
IT'S THE ANKOU...
I KNOW IT'S THE ANKOU!
LOOK, IT'S BEEN A LONG DAY. DID YOU HAVE AN APPOINTMENT? NO? SORRY!
CROC CROC
DAD... IT'S THE ANKOU.
SO WHAT?!
I THINK HE'S HERE... FOR YOU!

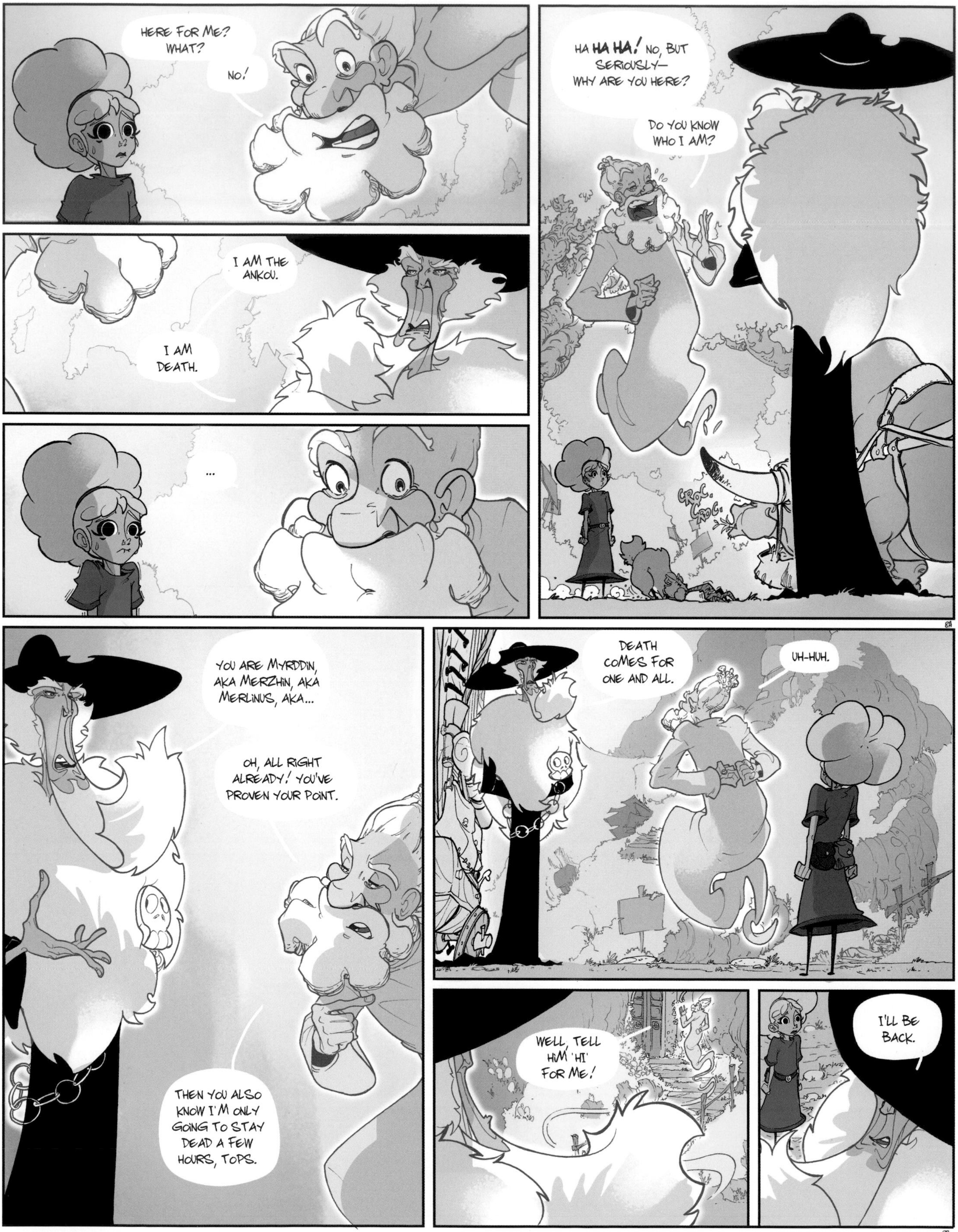
HERE FOR ME? WHAT?
NO!
I AM THE ANKOU.
I AM DEATH.
...
HA HA HA! NO, BUT SERIOUSLY— WHY ARE YOU HERE?
DO YOU KNOW WHO I AM?
CROC CROC
YOU ARE MYRDDIN, AKA MERZHIN, AKA MERLINUS, AKA...
OH, ALL RIGHT ALREADY! YOU'VE PROVEN YOUR POINT.
THEN YOU ALSO KNOW I'M ONLY GOING TO STAY DEAD A FEW HOURS, TOPS.
DEATH COMES FOR ONE AND ALL.
UH-HUH.
WELL, TELL HIM 'HI' FOR ME!
I'LL BE BACK.

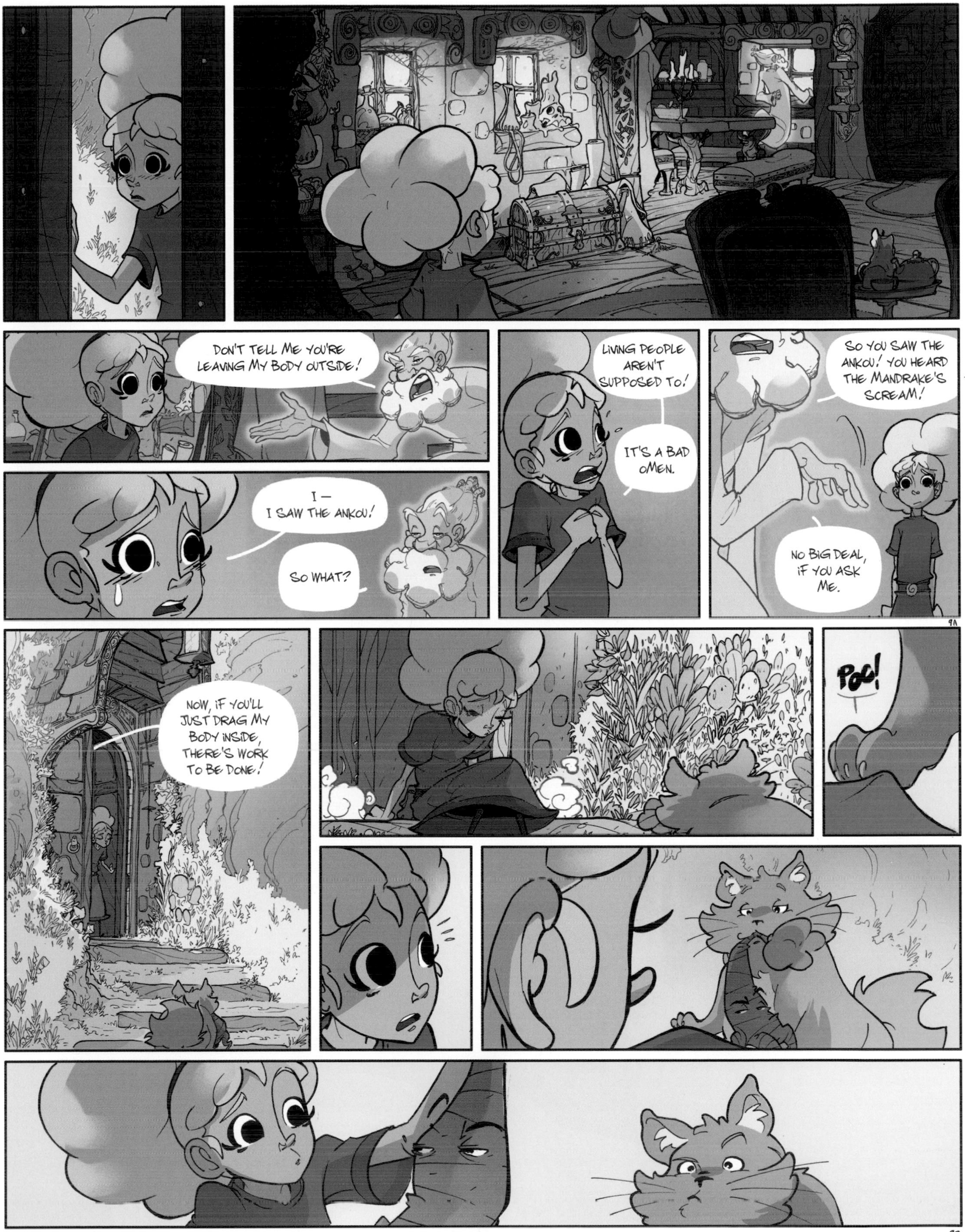

DON'T TELL ME YOU'RE LEAVING MY BODY OUTSIDE!
LIVING PEOPLE AREN'T SUPPOSED TO!
IT'S A BAD OMEN.
SO YOU SAW THE ANKOU! YOU HEARD THE MANDRAKE'S SCREAM!
NO BIG DEAL, IF YOU ASK ME.
I — I SAW THE ANKOU!
SO WHAT?
NOW, IF YOU'LL JUST DRAG MY BODY INSIDE, THERE'S WORK TO BE DONE!
POC!

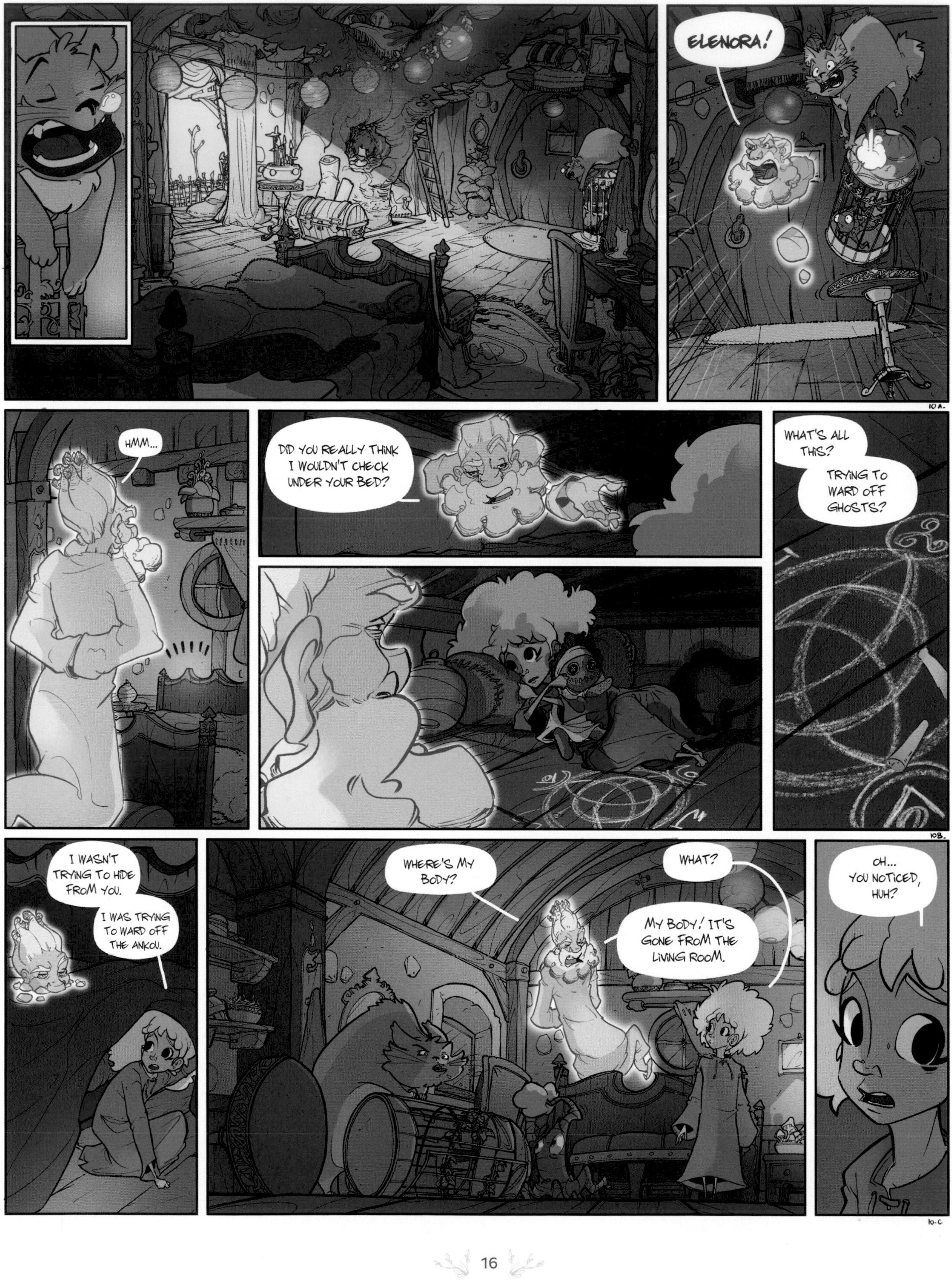

ELENORA!
HMM...
DID YOU REALLY THINK I WOULDN'T CHECK UNDER YOUR BED?
WHAT'S ALL THIS?
TRYING TO WARD OFF GHOSTS?
I WASN'T TRYING TO HIDE FROM YOU.
I WAS TRYING TO WARD OFF THE ANKOU.
WHERE'S MY BODY?
WHAT?
MY BODY! IT'S GONE FROM THE LIVING ROOM.
OH... YOU NOTICED, HUH?

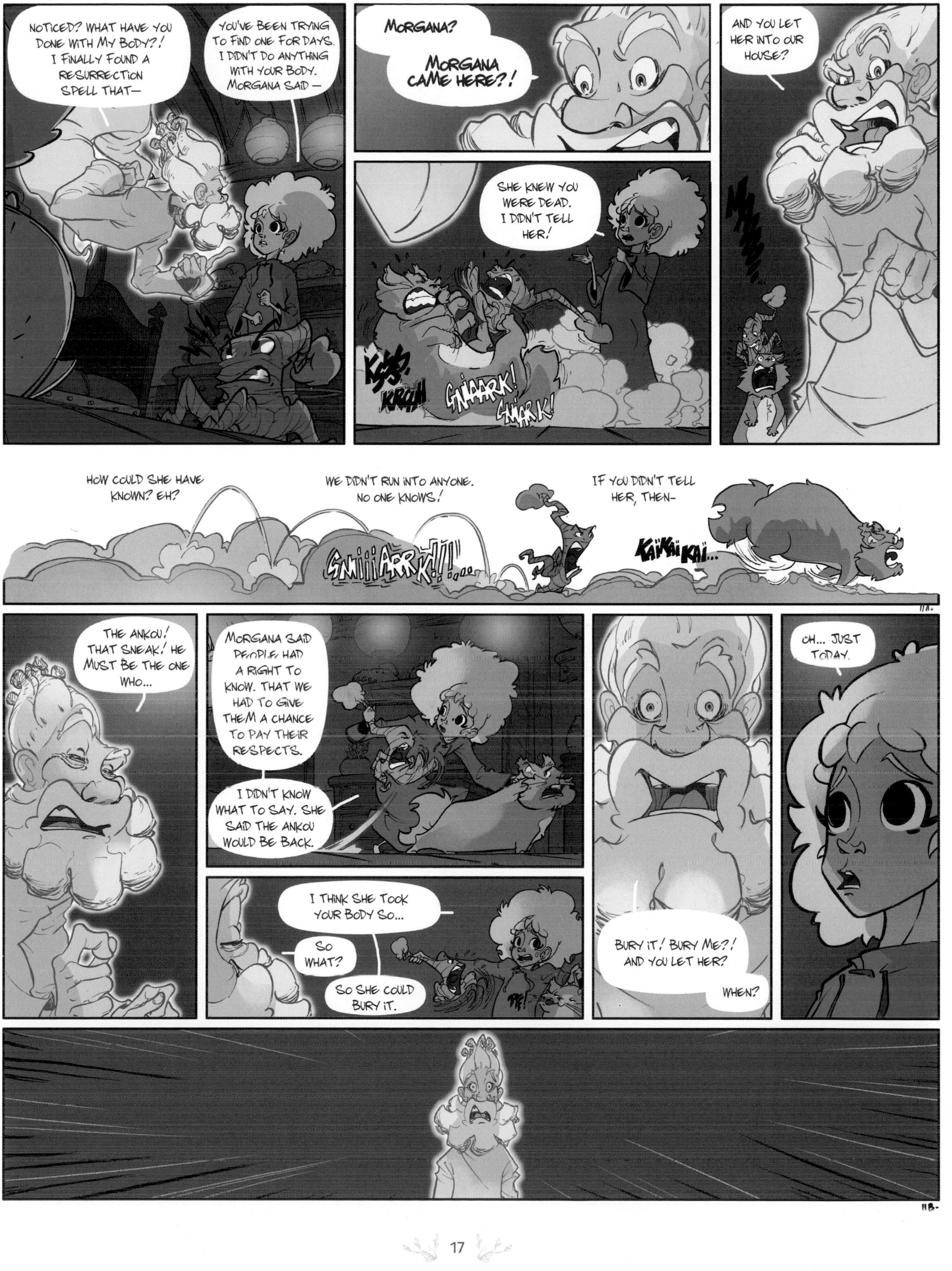
NOTICED? WHAT HAVE YOU DONE WITH MY BODY?! I FINALLY FOUND A RESURRECTION SPELL THAT—
YOU'VE BEEN TRYING TO FIND ONE FOR DAYS. I DIDN'T DO ANYTHING WITH YOUR BODY. MORGANA SAID—
MORGANA?
MORGANA CAME HERE?!
SHE KNEW YOU WERE DEAD. I DIDN'T TELL HER!
KRAH
GNIAARK!
GNIARK!
AND YOU LET HER INTO OUR HOUSE?
HOW COULD SHE HAVE KNOWN? EH?
WE DIDN'T RUN INTO ANYONE. NO ONE KNOWS!
GNIIIARRK!!!...
IF YOU DIDN'T TELL HER, THEN—
KAÏ KAÏ KAÏ...
THE ANKOU! THAT SNEAK! HE MUST BE THE ONE WHO...
MORGANA SAID PEOPLE HAD A RIGHT TO KNOW. THAT WE HAD TO GIVE THEM A CHANCE TO PAY THEIR RESPECTS.
I DIDN'T KNOW WHAT TO SAY. SHE SAID THE ANKOU WOULD BE BACK.
I THINK SHE TOOK YOUR BODY SO...
SO WHAT?
SO SHE COULD BURY IT.
PF!
BURY IT! BURY ME?! AND YOU LET HER?
WHEN?
OH... JUST TODAY.

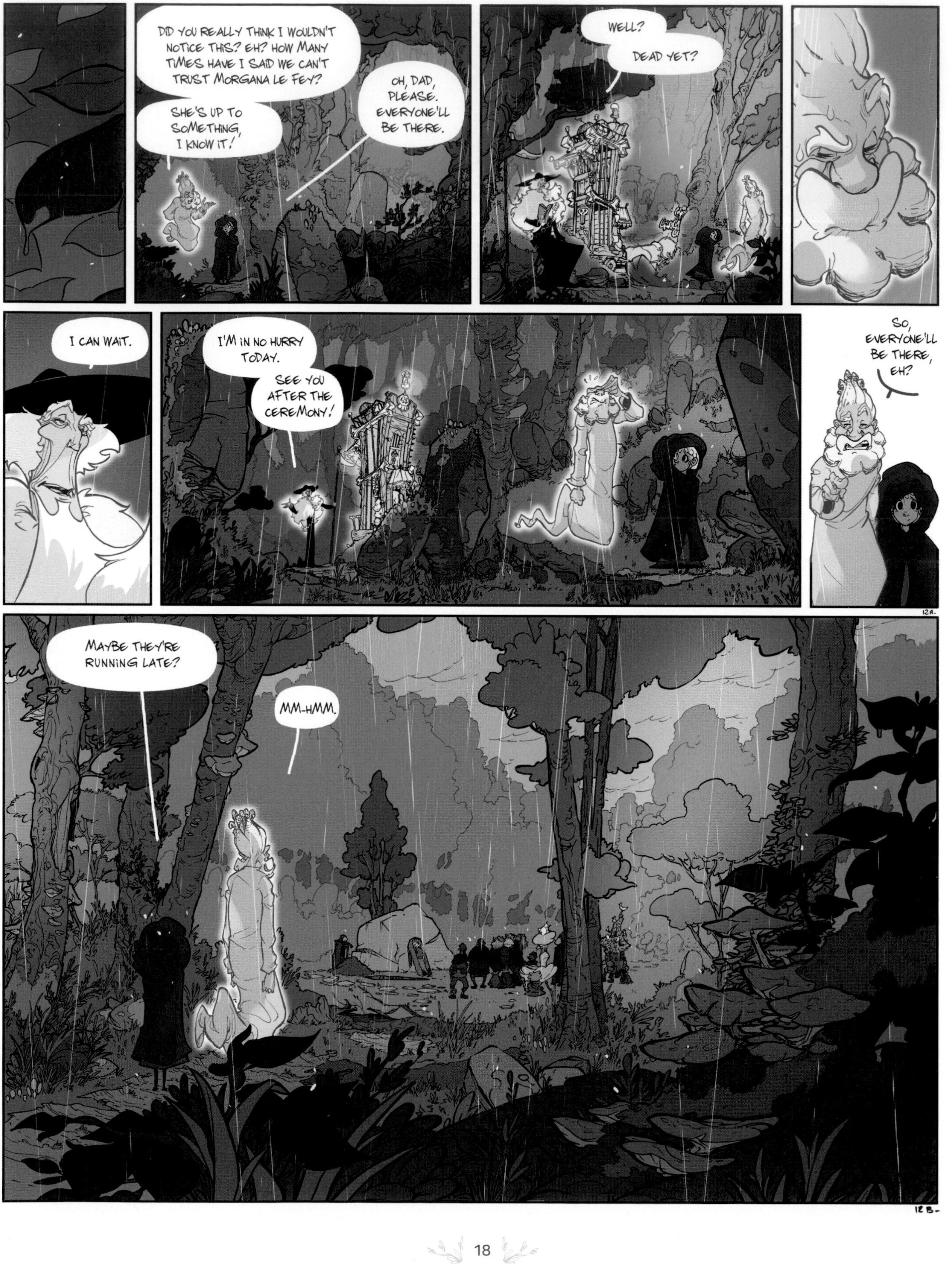
DID YOU REALLY THINK I WOULDN'T NOTICE THIS? EH? HOW MANY TIMES HAVE I SAID WE CAN'T TRUST MORGANA LE FEY?
SHE'S UP TO SOMETHING, I KNOW IT!
OH, DAD, PLEASE. EVERYONE'LL BE THERE.
WELL?
DEAD YET?
I CAN WAIT.
I'M IN NO HURRY TODAY.
SEE YOU AFTER THE CEREMONY!
SO, EVERYONE'LL BE THERE, EH?
MAYBE THEY'RE RUNNING LATE?
MM-HMM.

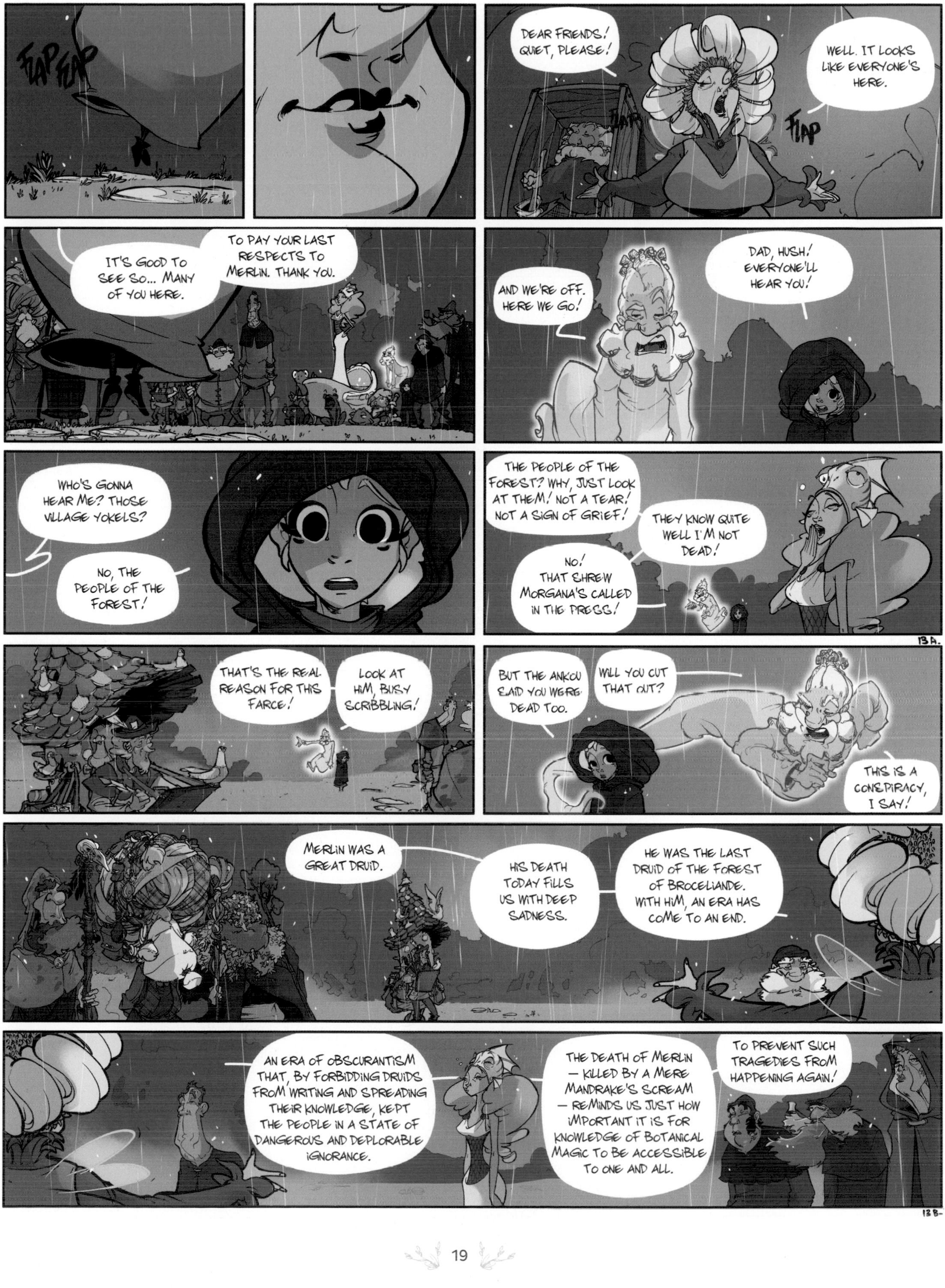
FLAP FLAP
DEAR FRIENDS! QUIET, PLEASE!
FLAP
WELL. IT LOOKS LIKE EVERYONE'S HERE.
FLAP
IT'S GOOD TO SEE SO... MANY OF YOU HERE.
TO PAY YOUR LAST RESPECTS TO MERLIN. THANK YOU.
AND WE'RE OFF. HERE WE GO!
DAD, HUSH! EVERYONE'LL HEAR YOU!
WHO'S GONNA HEAR ME? THOSE VILLAGE YOKELS?
NO, THE PEOPLE OF THE FOREST!
THE PEOPLE OF THE FOREST? WHY, JUST LOOK AT THEM! NOT A TEAR! NOT A SIGN OF GRIEF!
THEY KNOW QUITE WELL I'M NOT DEAD!
NO! THAT SHREW MORGANA'S CALLED IN THE PRESS!
13 A.
THAT'S THE REAL REASON FOR THIS FARCE!
LOOK AT HIM, BUSY SCRIBBLING!
BUT THE ANKOU SAID YOU WERE DEAD TOO.
WILL YOU CUT THAT OUT?
THIS IS A CONSPIRACY, I SAY!
MERLIN WAS A GREAT DRUID.
HIS DEATH TODAY FILLS US WITH DEEP SADNESS.
HE WAS THE LAST DRUID OF THE FOREST OF BROCELIANDE. WITH HIM, AN ERA HAS COME TO AN END.
AN ERA OF OBSCURANTISM THAT, BY FORBIDDING DRUIDS FROM WRITING AND SPREADING THEIR KNOWLEDGE, KEPT THE PEOPLE IN A STATE OF DANGEROUS AND DEPLORABLE IGNORANCE.
THE DEATH OF MERLIN — KILLED BY A MERE MANDRAKE'S SCREAM — REMINDS US JUST HOW IMPORTANT IT IS FOR KNOWLEDGE OF BOTANICAL MAGIC TO BE ACCESSIBLE TO ONE AND ALL.
TO PREVENT SUCH TRAGEDIES FROM HAPPENING AGAIN!
13 B-

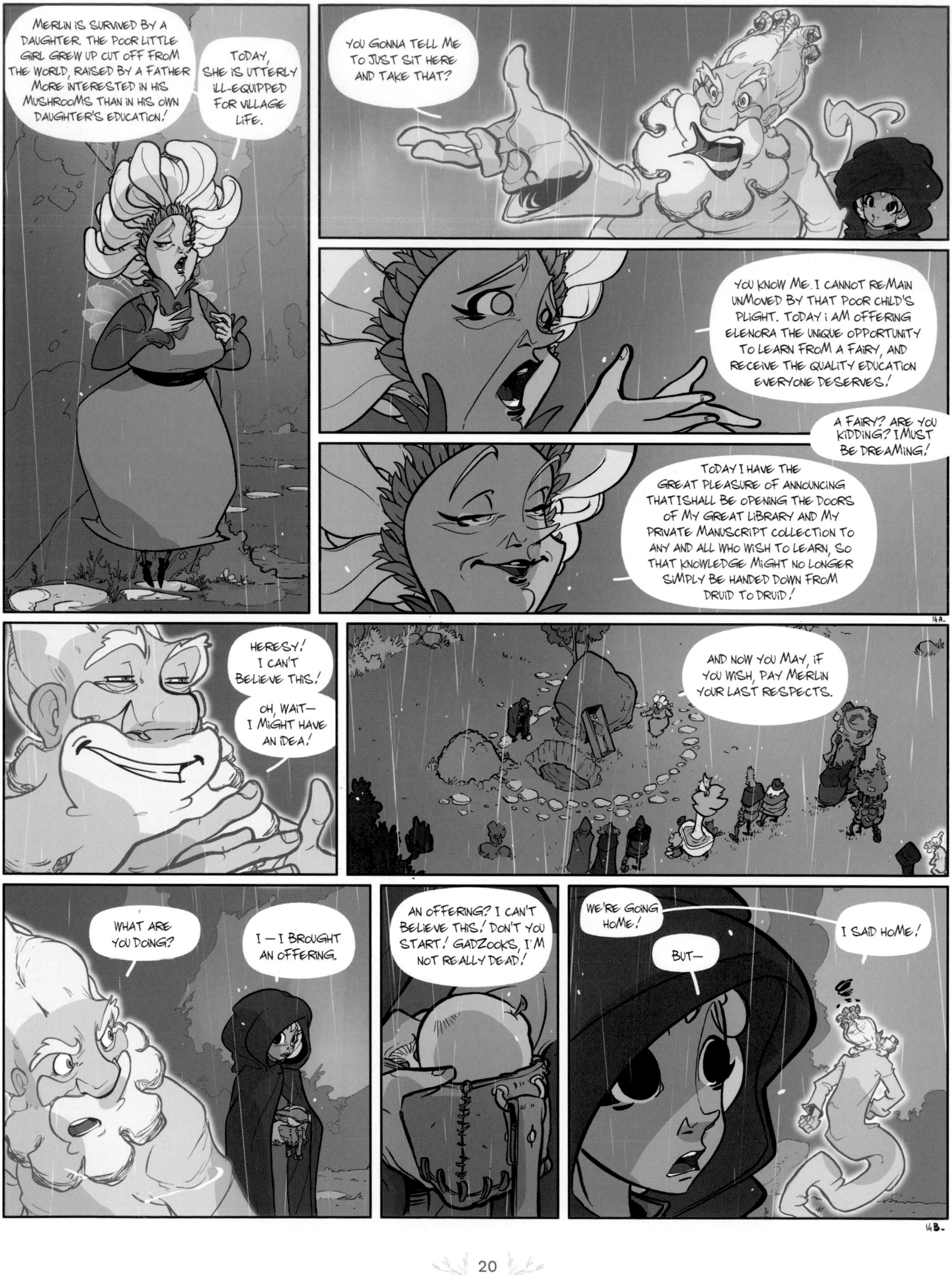

MERLIN IS SURVIVED BY A DAUGHTER. THE POOR LITTLE GIRL GREW UP CUT OFF FROM THE WORLD, RAISED BY A FATHER MORE INTERESTED IN HIS MUSHROOMS THAN IN HIS OWN DAUGHTER'S EDUCATION!
TODAY, SHE IS UTTERLY ILL-EQUIPPED FOR VILLAGE LIFE.
YOU GONNA TELL ME TO JUST SIT HERE AND TAKE THAT?
YOU KNOW ME. I CANNOT REMAIN UNMOVED BY THAT POOR CHILD'S PLIGHT. TODAY I AM OFFERING ELENORA THE UNIQUE OPPORTUNITY TO LEARN FROM A FAIRY, AND RECEIVE THE QUALITY EDUCATION EVERYONE DESERVES!
A FAIRY? ARE YOU KIDDING? I MUST BE DREAMING!
TODAY I HAVE THE GREAT PLEASURE OF ANNOUNCING THAT I SHALL BE OPENING THE DOORS OF MY GREAT LIBRARY AND MY PRIVATE MANUSCRIPT COLLECTION TO ANY AND ALL WHO WISH TO LEARN, SO THAT KNOWLEDGE MIGHT NO LONGER SIMPLY BE HANDED DOWN FROM DRUID TO DRUID!
HERESY! I CAN'T BELIEVE THIS!
OH, WAIT— I MIGHT HAVE AN IDEA!
AND NOW YOU MAY, IF YOU WISH, PAY MERLIN YOUR LAST RESPECTS.
WHAT ARE YOU DOING?
I—I BROUGHT AN OFFERING.
AN OFFERING? I CAN'T BELIEVE THIS! DON'T YOU START! GADZOOKS, I'M NOT REALLY DEAD!
WE'RE GOING HOME!
BUT—
I SAID HOME!

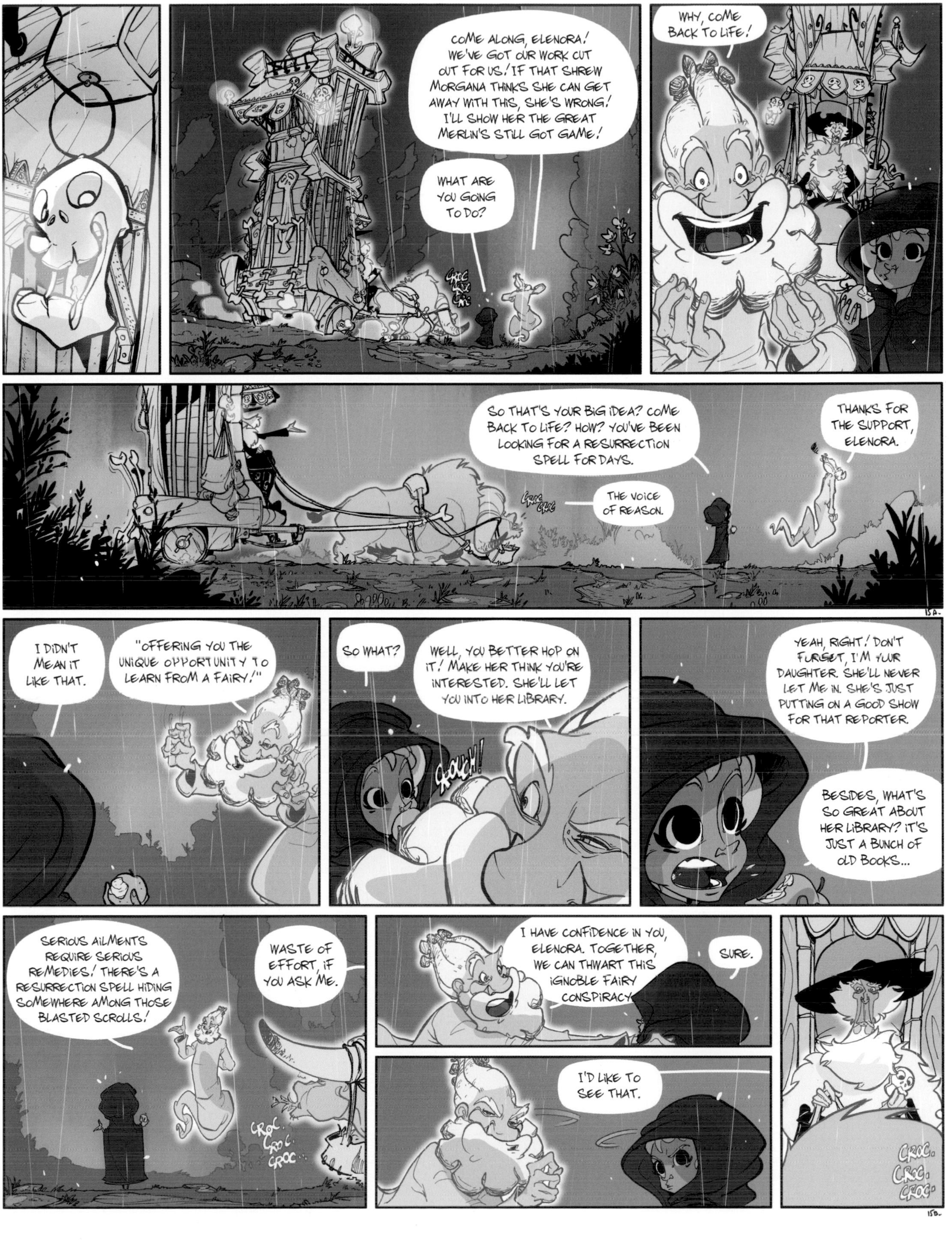
COME ALONG, ELENORA! WE'VE GOT OUR WORK CUT OUT FOR US! IF THAT SHREW MORGANA THINKS SHE CAN GET AWAY WITH THIS, SHE'S WRONG! I'LL SHOW HER THE GREAT MERLIN'S STILL GOT GAME!
WHAT ARE YOU GOING TO DO?
WHY, COME BACK TO LIFE!
SO THAT'S YOUR BIG IDEA? COME BACK TO LIFE? HOW? YOU'VE BEEN LOOKING FOR A RESURRECTION SPELL FOR DAYS.
THANKS FOR THE SUPPORT, ELENORA.
THE VOICE OF REASON.
I DIDN'T MEAN IT LIKE THAT.
"OFFERING YOU THE UNIQUE OPPORTUNITY TO LEARN FROM A FAIRY!"
SO WHAT?
WELL, YOU BETTER HOP ON IT! MAKE HER THINK YOU'RE INTERESTED. SHE'LL LET YOU INTO HER LIBRARY.
YEAH, RIGHT! DON'T FORGET, I'M YOUR DAUGHTER. SHE'LL NEVER LET ME IN. SHE'S JUST PUTTING ON A GOOD SHOW FOR THAT REPORTER.
BESIDES, WHAT'S SO GREAT ABOUT HER LIBRARY? IT'S JUST A BUNCH OF OLD BOOKS...
SERIOUS AILMENTS REQUIRE SERIOUS REMEDIES! THERE'S A RESURRECTION SPELL HIDING SOMEWHERE AMONG THOSE BLASTED SCROLLS!
WASTE OF EFFORT, IF YOU ASK ME.
CROC. CROC. CROC.
I HAVE CONFIDENCE IN YOU, ELENORA. TOGETHER, WE CAN THWART THIS IGNOBLE FAIRY CONSPIRACY.
SURE.
I'D LIKE TO SEE THAT.
CROC. CROC. CROC.

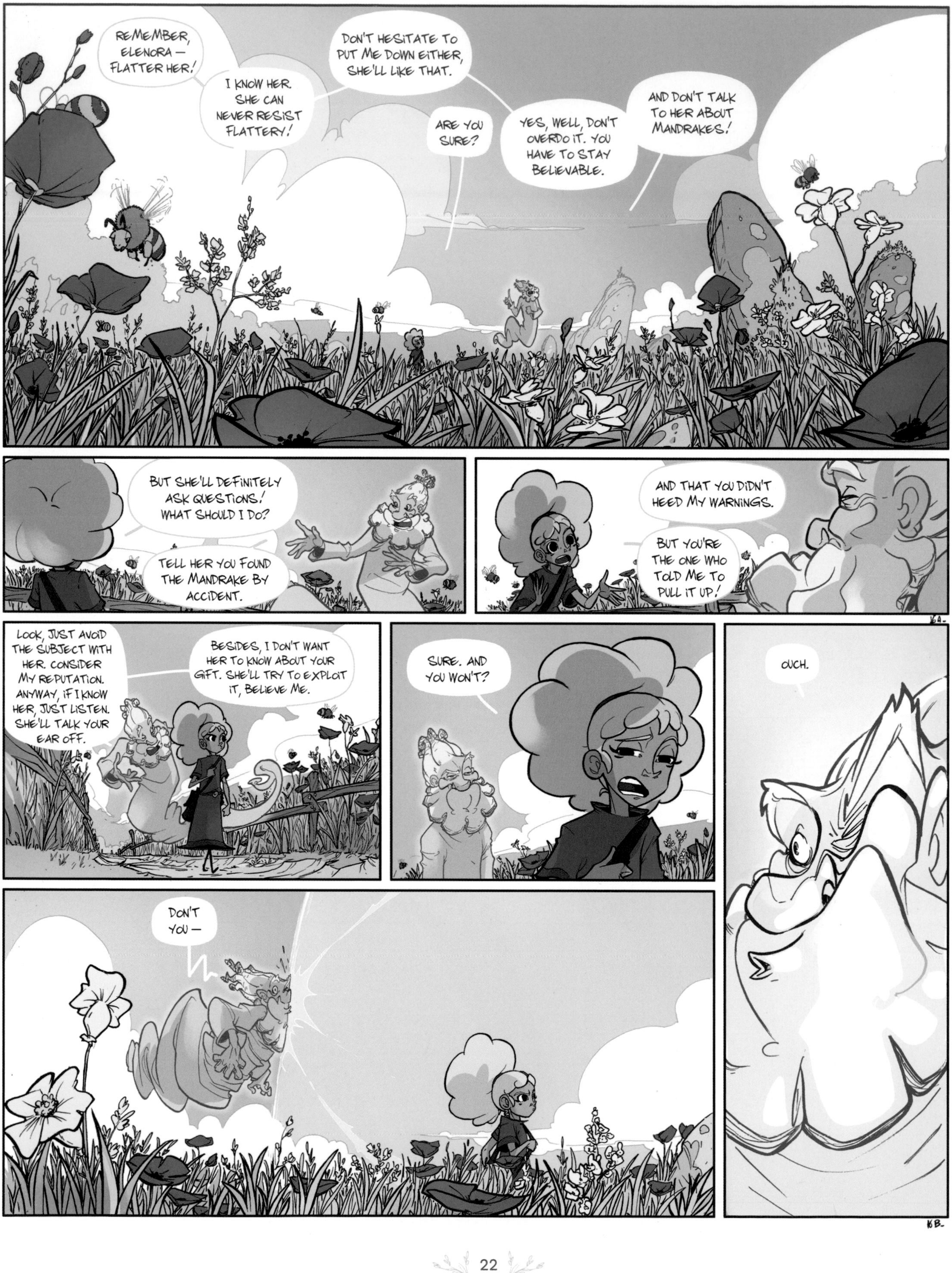
REMEMBER, ELENORA — FLATTER HER!
I KNOW HER. SHE CAN NEVER RESIST FLATTERY!
DON'T HESITATE TO PUT ME DOWN EITHER, SHE'LL LIKE THAT.
ARE YOU SURE?
YES, WELL, DON'T OVERDO IT. YOU HAVE TO STAY BELIEVABLE.
AND DON'T TALK TO HER ABOUT MANDRAKES!
BUT SHE'LL DEFINITELY ASK QUESTIONS! WHAT SHOULD I DO?
TELL HER YOU FOUND THE MANDRAKE BY ACCIDENT.
AND THAT YOU DIDN'T HEED MY WARNINGS.
BUT YOU'RE THE ONE WHO TOLD ME TO PULL IT UP!
LOOK, JUST AVOID THE SUBJECT WITH HER. CONSIDER MY REPUTATION. ANYWAY, IF I KNOW HER, JUST LISTEN. SHE'LL TALK YOUR EAR OFF.
BESIDES, I DON'T WANT HER TO KNOW ABOUT YOUR GIFT. SHE'LL TRY TO EXPLOIT IT, BELIEVE ME.
SURE. AND YOU WON'T?
OUCH.
DON'T YOU —

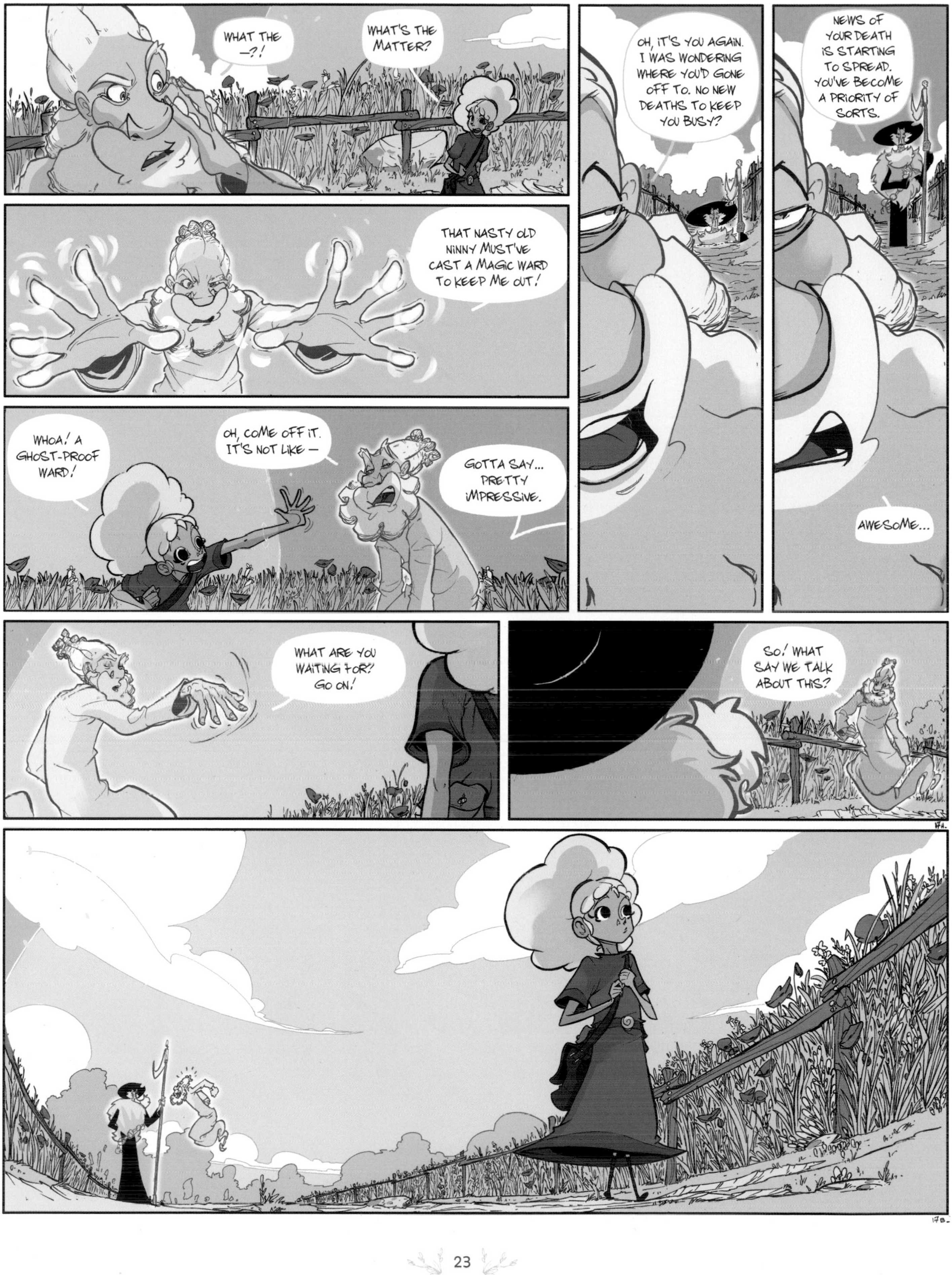
WHAT THE —?!
WHAT'S THE MATTER?
OH, IT'S YOU AGAIN. I WAS WONDERING WHERE YOU'D GONE OFF TO. NO NEW DEATHS TO KEEP YOU BUSY?
NEWS OF YOUR DEATH IS STARTING TO SPREAD. YOU'VE BECOME A PRIORITY OF SORTS.
THAT NASTY OLD NINNY MUST'VE CAST A MAGIC WARD TO KEEP ME OUT!
WHOA! A GHOST-PROOF WARD!
OH, COME OFF IT. IT'S NOT LIKE —
GOTTA SAY... PRETTY IMPRESSIVE.
AWESOME...
WHAT ARE YOU WAITING FOR? GO ON!
SO! WHAT SAY WE TALK ABOUT THIS?

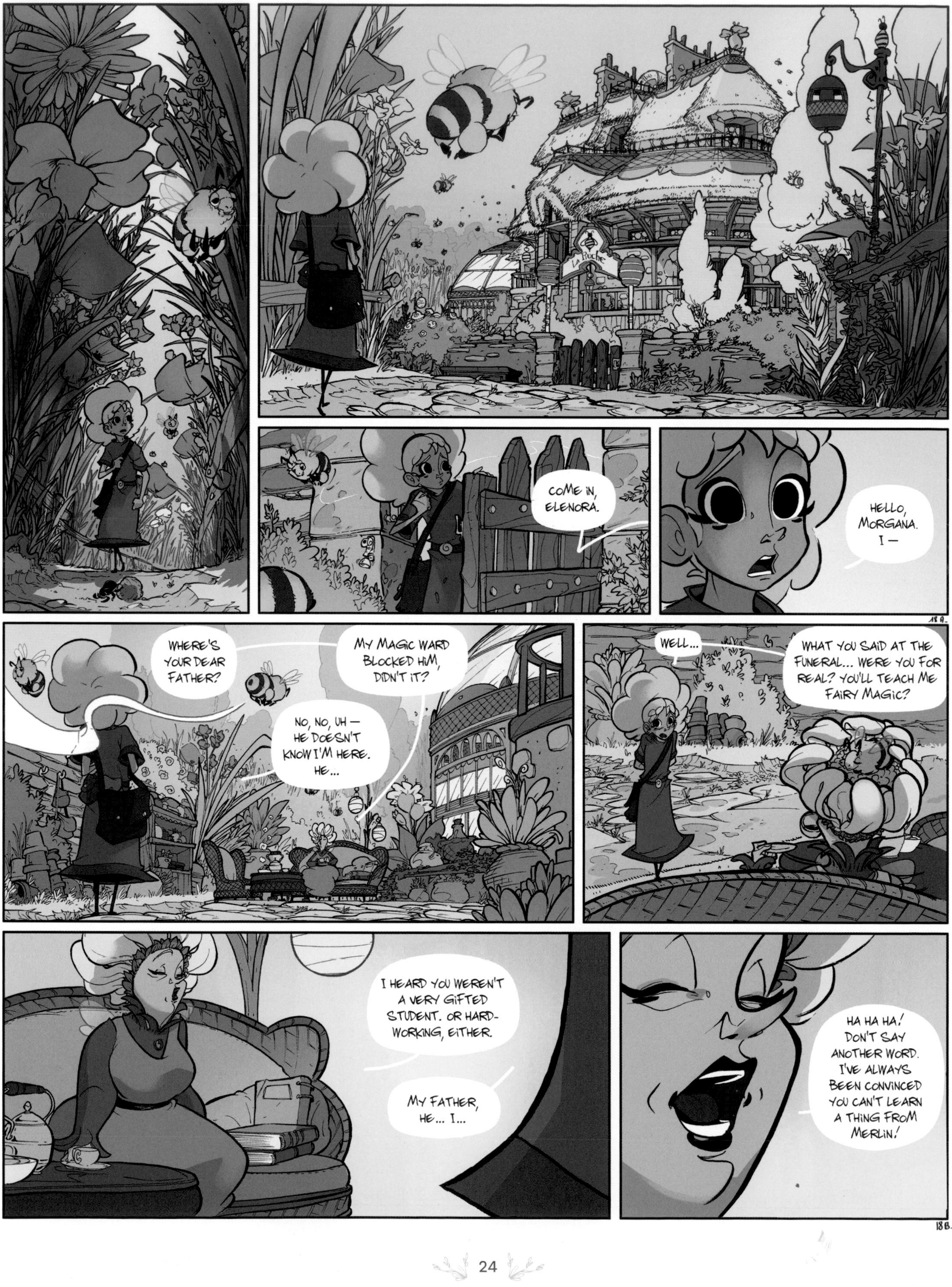

La Ruche
COME IN, ELENORA.
HELLO, MORGANA. I —
WHERE'S YOUR DEAR FATHER?
MY MAGIC WARD BLOCKED HIM, DIDN'T IT?
NO, NO, UH — HE DOESN'T KNOW I'M HERE. HE...
WELL...
WHAT YOU SAID AT THE FUNERAL... WERE YOU FOR REAL? YOU'LL TEACH ME FAIRY MAGIC?
I HEARD YOU WEREN'T A VERY GIFTED STUDENT. OR HARD-WORKING, EITHER.
MY FATHER, HE... I...
HA HA HA! DON'T SAY ANOTHER WORD. I'VE ALWAYS BEEN CONVINCED YOU CAN'T LEARN A THING FROM MERLIN!

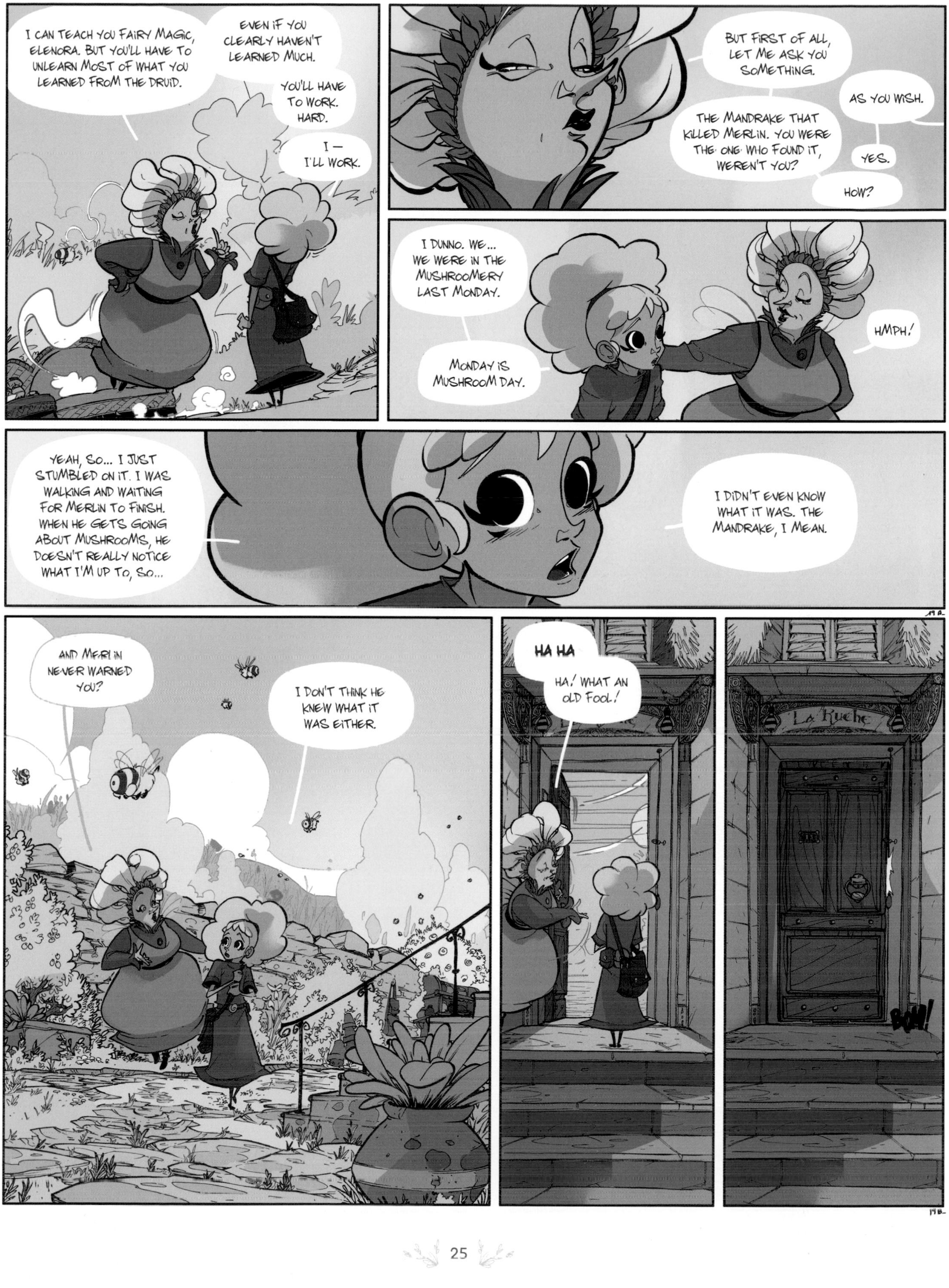
I CAN TEACH YOU FAIRY MAGIC, ELENORA. BUT YOU'LL HAVE TO UNLEARN MOST OF WHAT YOU LEARNED FROM THE DRUID.
EVEN IF YOU CLEARLY HAVEN'T LEARNED MUCH.
YOU'LL HAVE TO WORK. HARD.
I — I'LL WORK.
BUT FIRST OF ALL, LET ME ASK YOU SOMETHING.
AS YOU WISH.
THE MANDRAKE THAT KILLED MERLIN. YOU WERE THE ONE WHO FOUND IT, WEREN'T YOU?
YES.
HOW?
I DUNNO. WE... WE WERE IN THE MUSHROOMERY LAST MONDAY.
MONDAY IS MUSHROOM DAY.
HMPH!
YEAH, SO... I JUST STUMBLED ON IT. I WAS WALKING AND WAITING FOR MERLIN TO FINISH. WHEN HE GETS GOING ABOUT MUSHROOMS, HE DOESN'T REALLY NOTICE WHAT I'M UP TO, SO...
I DIDN'T EVEN KNOW WHAT IT WAS. THE MANDRAKE, I MEAN.
AND MERLIN NEVER WARNED YOU?
I DON'T THINK HE KNEW WHAT IT WAS EITHER.
HA HA
HA! WHAT AN OLD FOOL!
La Ruche
BOM!

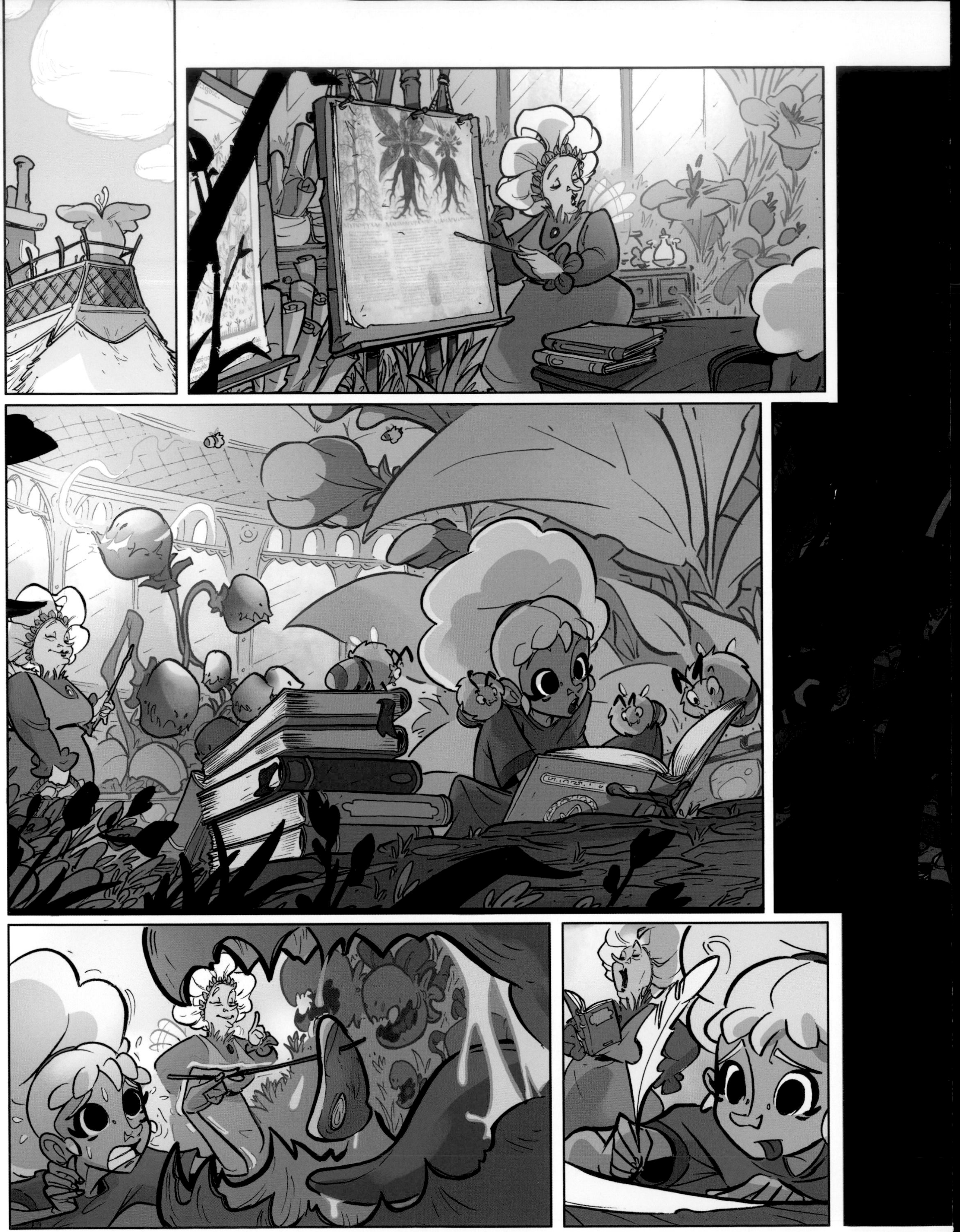

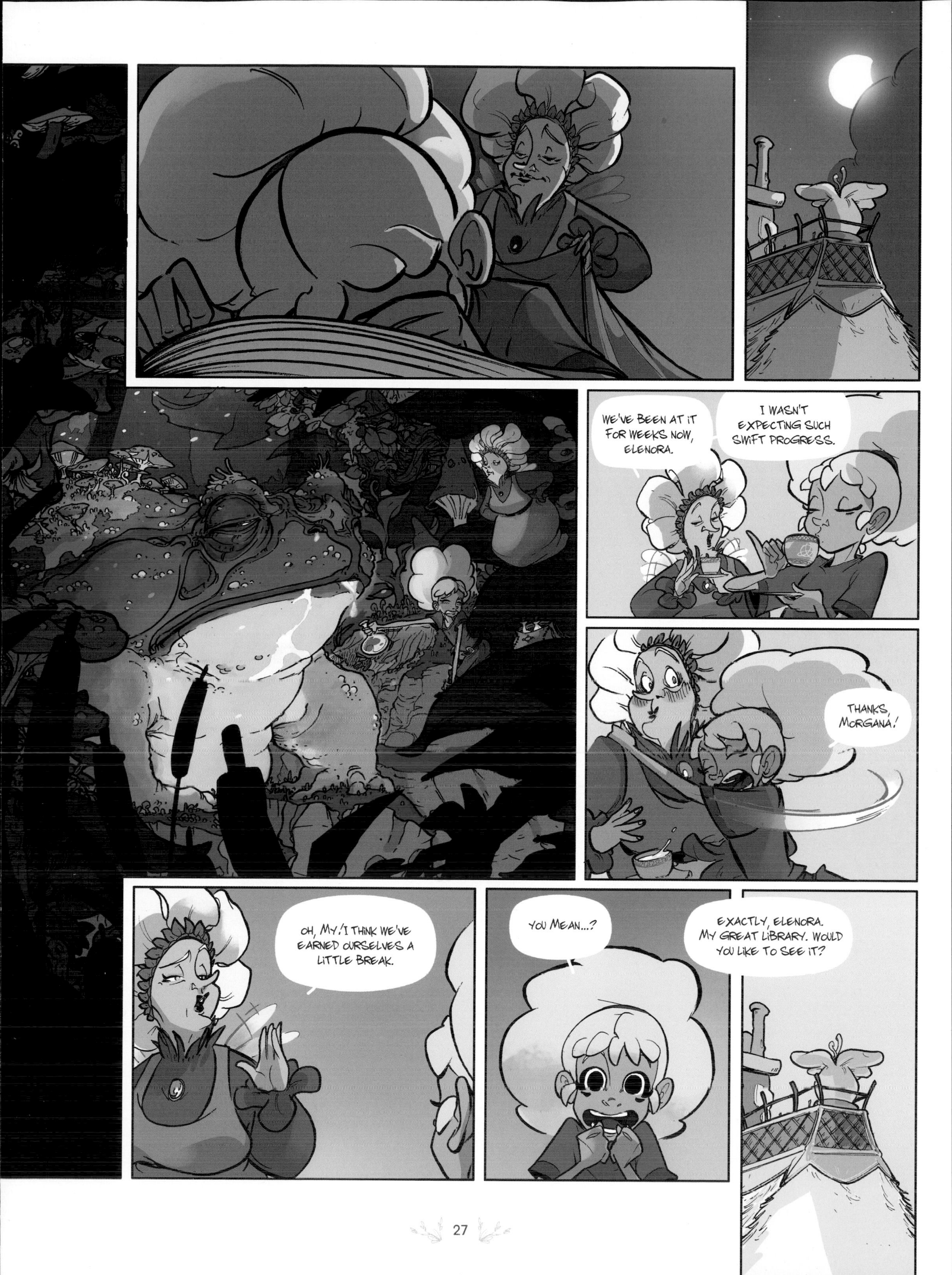
WE'VE BEEN AT IT FOR WEEKS NOW, ELENORA.
I WASN'T EXPECTING SUCH SWIFT PROGRESS.
THANKS, MORGANA!
OH, MY! I THINK WE'VE EARNED OURSELVES A LITTLE BREAK.
YOU MEAN...?
EXACTLY, ELENORA. MY GREAT LIBRARY. WOULD YOU LIKE TO SEE IT?

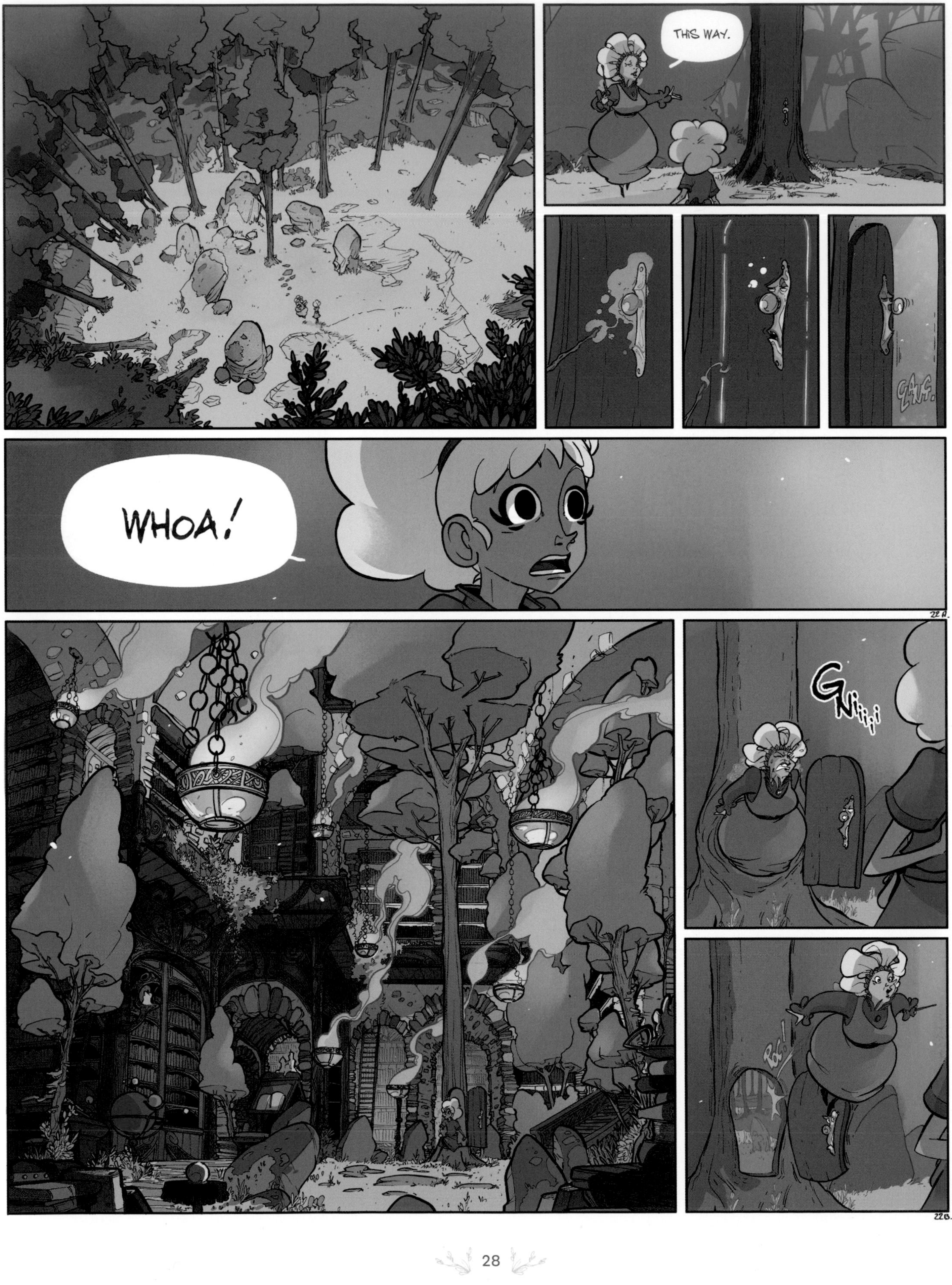
THIS WAY.
CLANG.
WHOA!
GNiiii
POC!

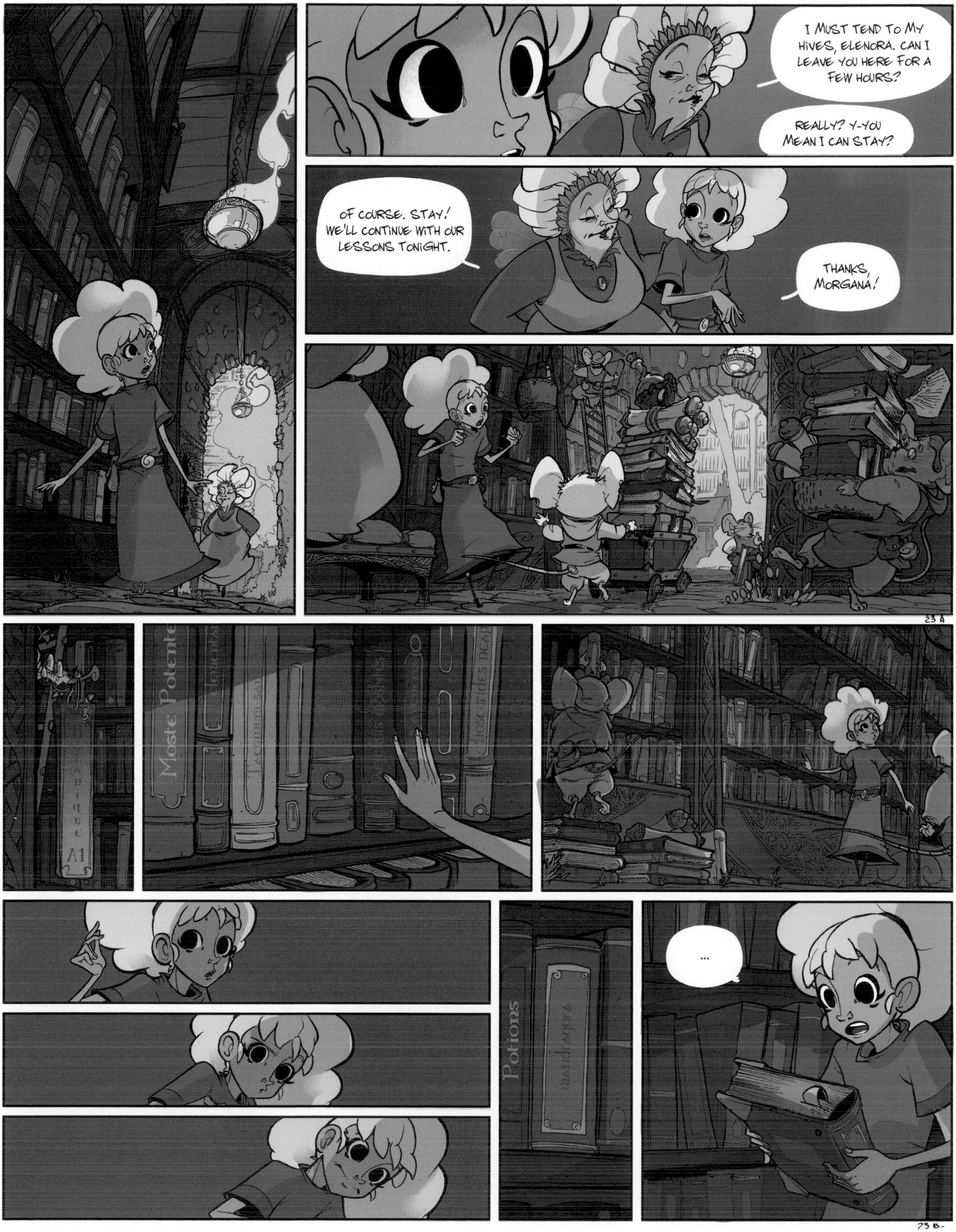
I MUST TEND TO MY HIVES, ELENORA. CAN I LEAVE YOU HERE FOR A FEW HOURS?
REALLY? Y-YOU MEAN I CAN STAY?
OF COURSE. STAY! WE'LL CONTINUE WITH OUR LESSONS TONIGHT.
THANKS, MORGANA!
Moste Potente
A1
Potions
...

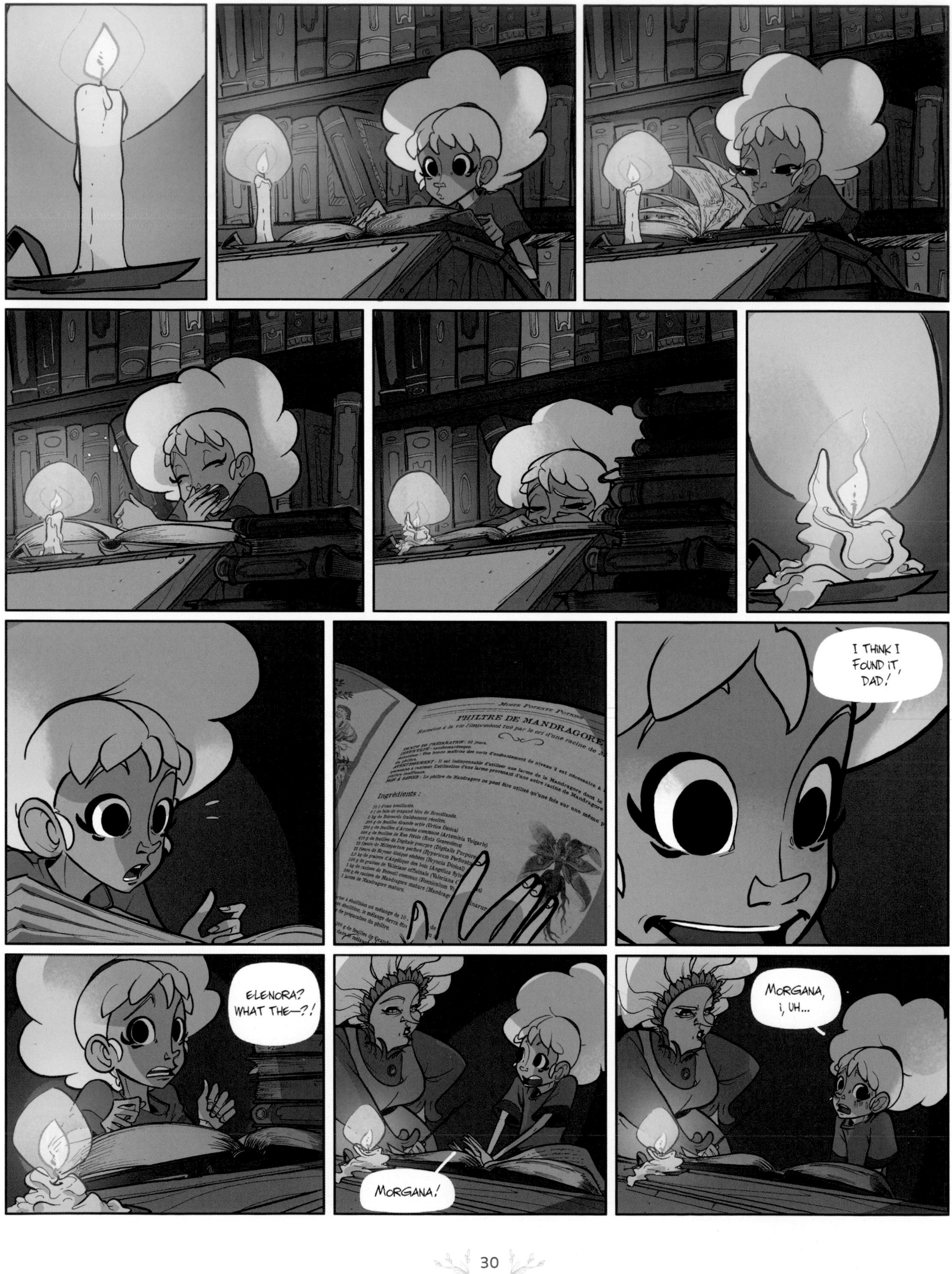
PHILTRE DE MANDRAGORE
Ingrédients :
I THINK I FOUND IT, DAD!
ELENORA? WHAT THE—?!
MORGANA!
MORGANA, I, UH...

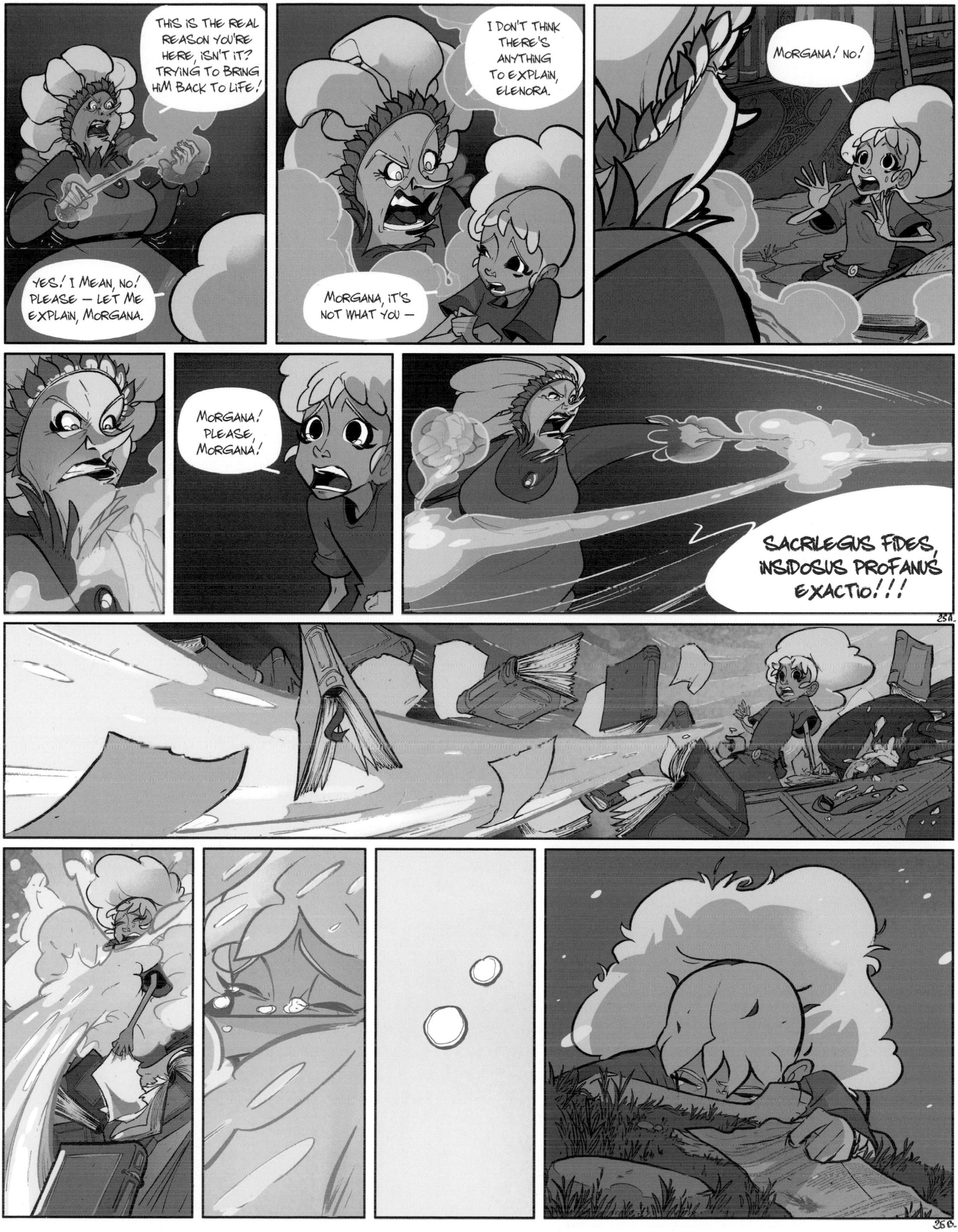
THIS IS THE REAL REASON YOU'RE HERE, ISN'T IT? TRYING TO BRING HIM BACK TO LIFE!
YES! I MEAN, NO! PLEASE — LET ME EXPLAIN, MORGANA.
I DON'T THINK THERE'S ANYTHING TO EXPLAIN, ELENORA.
MORGANA, IT'S NOT WHAT YOU —
MORGANA! NO!
MORGANA! PLEASE, MORGANA!
SACRILEGUS FIDES, INSIDOSUS PROFANUS EXACTIO!!!

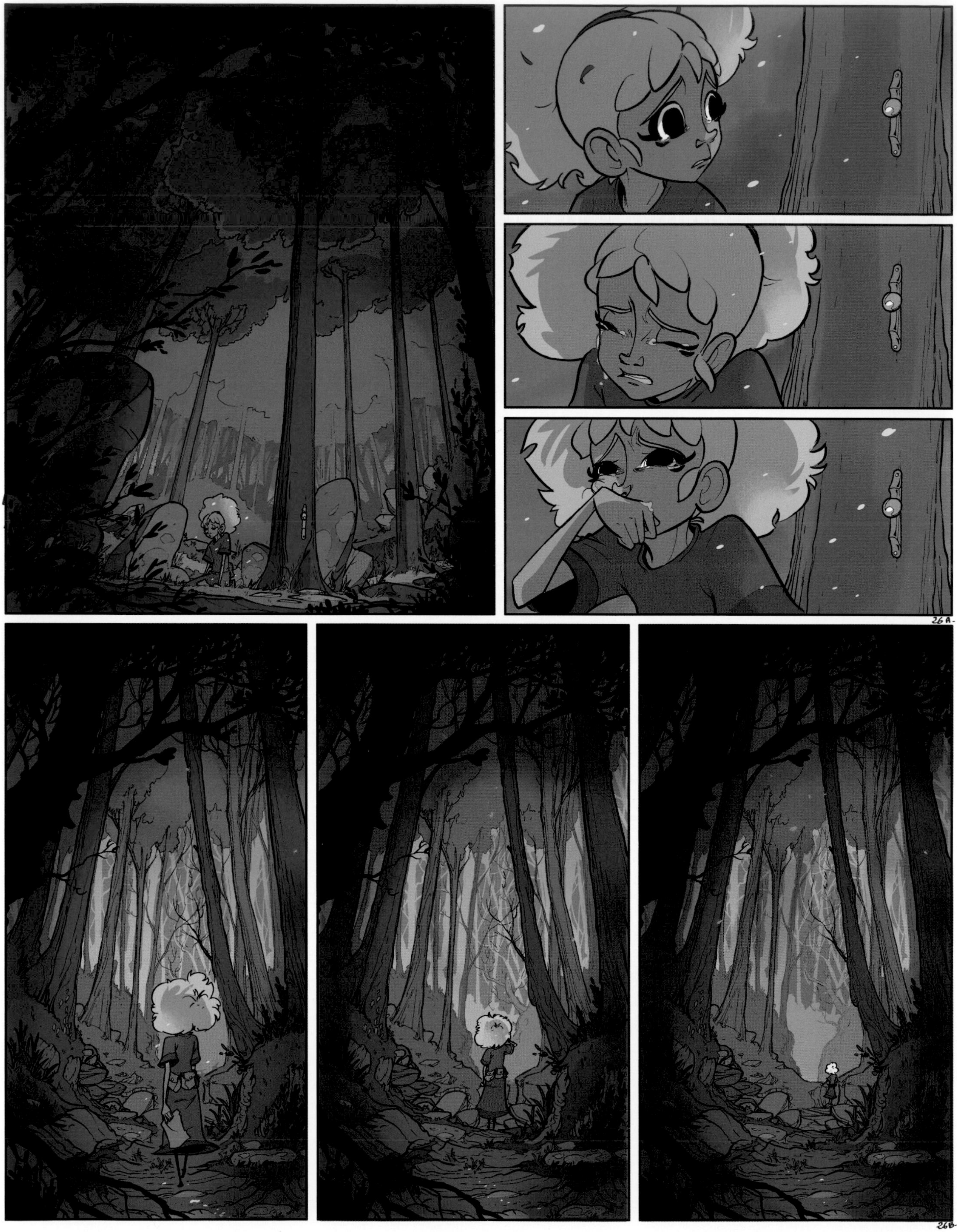
26A-
26B-

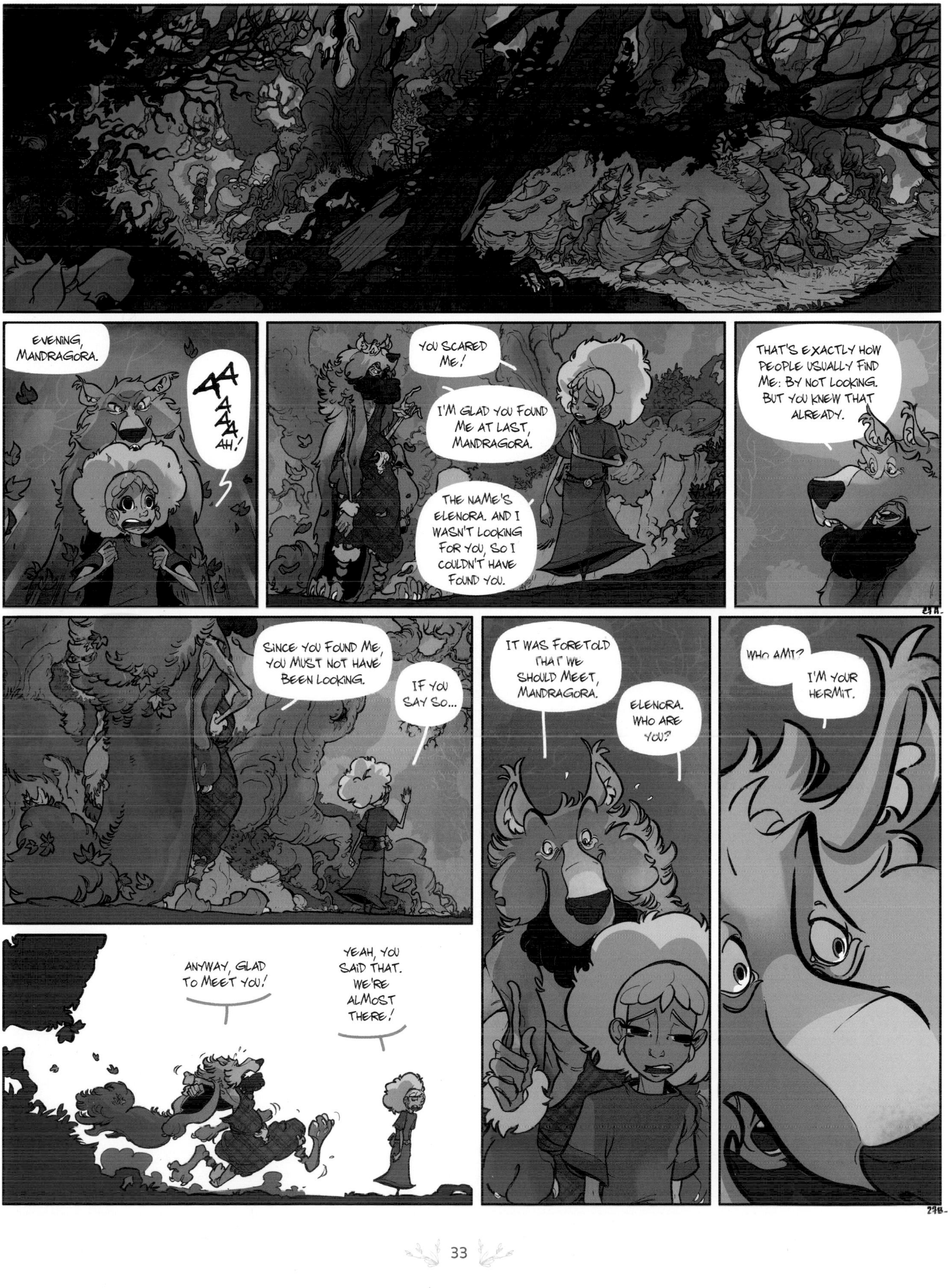

EVENING, MANDRAGORA.
AAAAAH!
YOU SCARED ME!
I'M GLAD YOU FOUND ME AT LAST, MANDRAGORA.
THE NAME'S ELENORA. AND I WASN'T LOOKING FOR YOU, SO I COULDN'T HAVE FOUND YOU.
THAT'S EXACTLY HOW PEOPLE USUALLY FIND ME: BY NOT LOOKING. BUT YOU KNEW THAT ALREADY.
SINCE YOU FOUND ME, YOU MUST NOT HAVE BEEN LOOKING.
IF YOU SAY SO...
IT WAS FORETOLD THAT WE SHOULD MEET, MANDRAGORA.
ELENORA. WHO ARE YOU?
WHO AM I?
I'M YOUR HERMIT.
ANYWAY, GLAD TO MEET YOU!
YEAH, YOU SAID THAT. WE'RE ALMOST THERE!

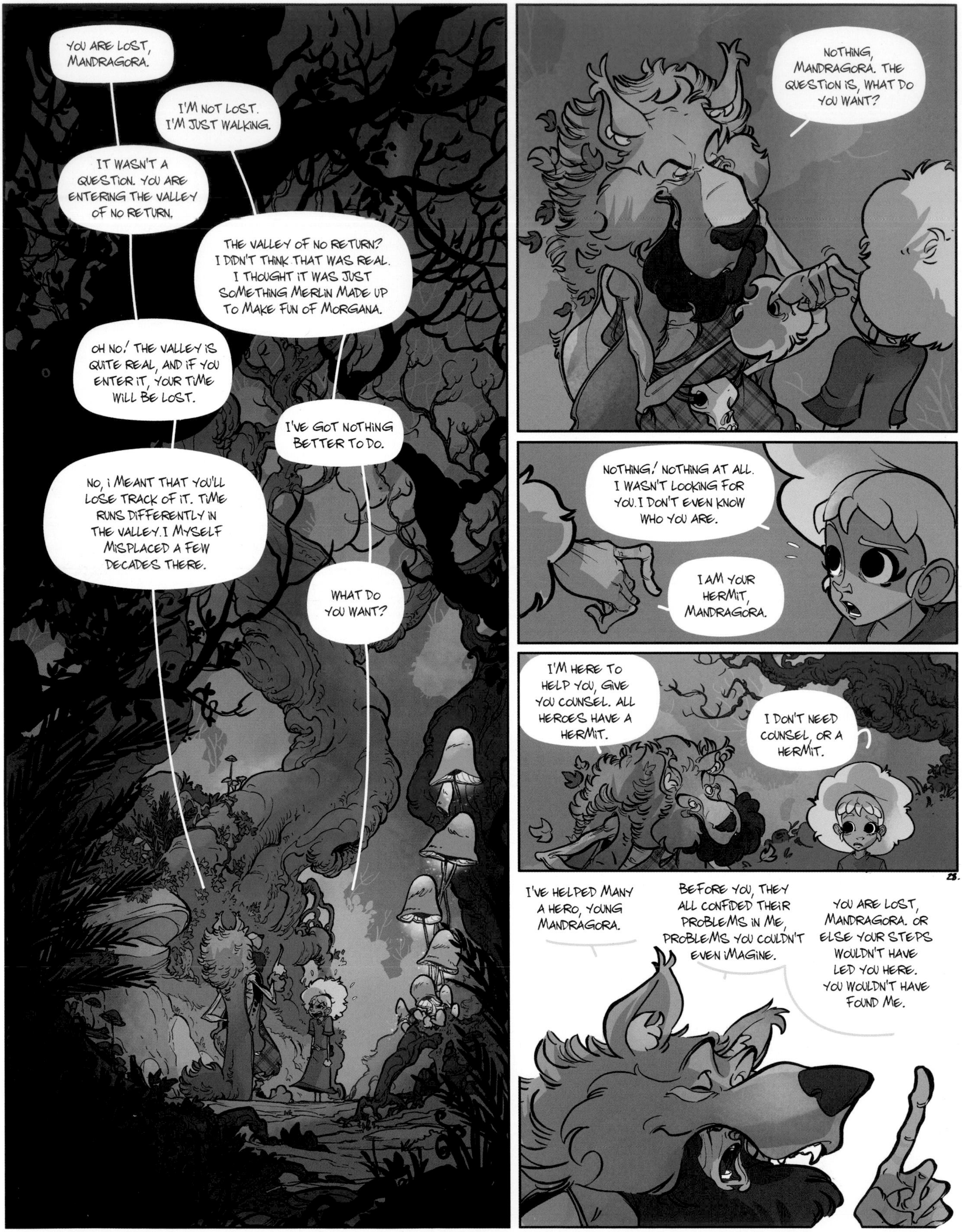
YOU ARE LOST, MANDRAGORA.
I'M NOT LOST. I'M JUST WALKING.
IT WASN'T A QUESTION. YOU ARE ENTERING THE VALLEY OF NO RETURN.
THE VALLEY OF NO RETURN? I DIDN'T THINK THAT WAS REAL. I THOUGHT IT WAS JUST SOMETHING MERLIN MADE UP TO MAKE FUN OF MORGANA.
OH NO! THE VALLEY IS QUITE REAL, AND IF YOU ENTER IT, YOUR TIME WILL BE LOST.
I'VE GOT NOTHING BETTER TO DO.
NO, I MEANT THAT YOU'LL LOSE TRACK OF IT. TIME RUNS DIFFERENTLY IN THE VALLEY. I MYSELF MISPLACED A FEW DECADES THERE.
WHAT DO YOU WANT?
NOTHING, MANDRAGORA. THE QUESTION IS, WHAT DO YOU WANT?
NOTHING! NOTHING AT ALL. I WASN'T LOOKING FOR YOU. I DON'T EVEN KNOW WHO YOU ARE.
I AM YOUR HERMIT, MANDRAGORA.
I'M HERE TO HELP YOU, GIVE YOU COUNSEL. ALL HEROES HAVE A HERMIT.
I DON'T NEED COUNSEL, OR A HERMIT.
I'VE HELPED MANY A HERO, YOUNG MANDRAGORA.
BEFORE YOU, THEY ALL CONFIDED THEIR PROBLEMS IN ME, PROBLEMS YOU COULDN'T EVEN IMAGINE.
YOU ARE LOST, MANDRAGORA. OR ELSE YOUR STEPS WOULDN'T HAVE LED YOU HERE. YOU WOULDN'T HAVE FOUND ME.

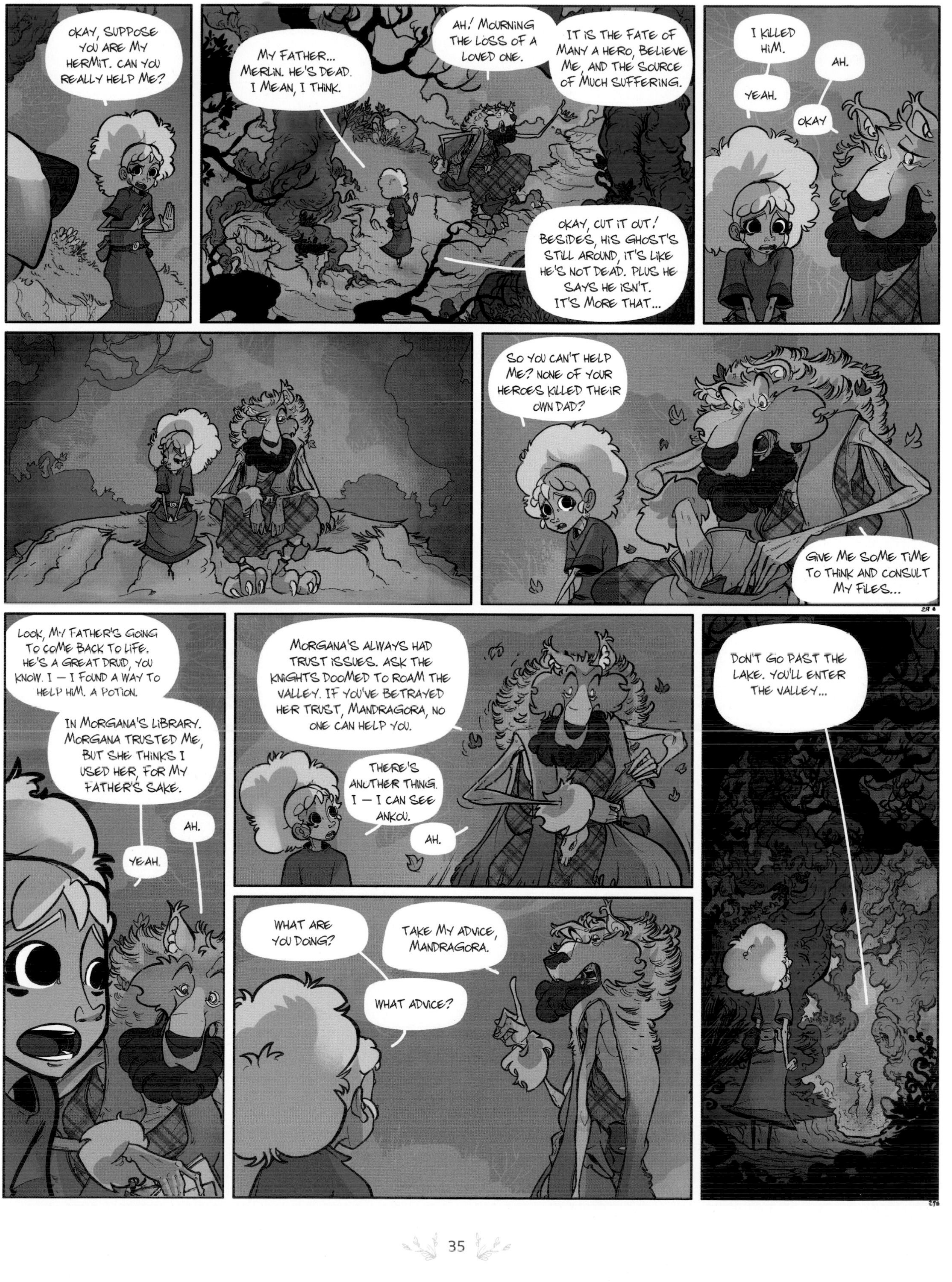
OKAY, SUPPOSE YOU ARE MY HERMIT. CAN YOU REALLY HELP ME?
MY FATHER... MERLIN. HE'S DEAD. I MEAN, I THINK.
AH! MOURNING THE LOSS OF A LOVED ONE.
IT IS THE FATE OF MANY A HERO, BELIEVE ME, AND THE SOURCE OF MUCH SUFFERING.
OKAY, CUT IT OUT! BESIDES, HIS GHOST'S STILL AROUND, IT'S LIKE HE'S NOT DEAD. PLUS HE SAYS HE ISN'T. IT'S MORE THAT...
I KILLED HIM.
AH.
YEAH.
OKAY
SO YOU CAN'T HELP ME? NONE OF YOUR HEROES KILLED THEIR OWN DAD?
GIVE ME SOME TIME TO THINK AND CONSULT MY FILES...
LOOK, MY FATHER'S GOING TO COME BACK TO LIFE. HE'S A GREAT DRUID, YOU KNOW. I — I FOUND A WAY TO HELP HIM. A POTION.
IN MORGANA'S LIBRARY. MORGANA TRUSTED ME, BUT SHE THINKS I USED HER, FOR MY FATHER'S SAKE.
AH.
YEAH.
MORGANA'S ALWAYS HAD TRUST ISSUES. ASK THE KNIGHTS DOOMED TO ROAM THE VALLEY. IF YOU'VE BETRAYED HER TRUST, MANDRAGORA, NO ONE CAN HELP YOU.
THERE'S ANOTHER THING. I — I CAN SEE ANKOU.
AH.
WHAT ARE YOU DOING?
TAKE MY ADVICE, MANDRAGORA.
WHAT ADVICE?
DON'T GO PAST THE LAKE. YOU'LL ENTER THE VALLEY...

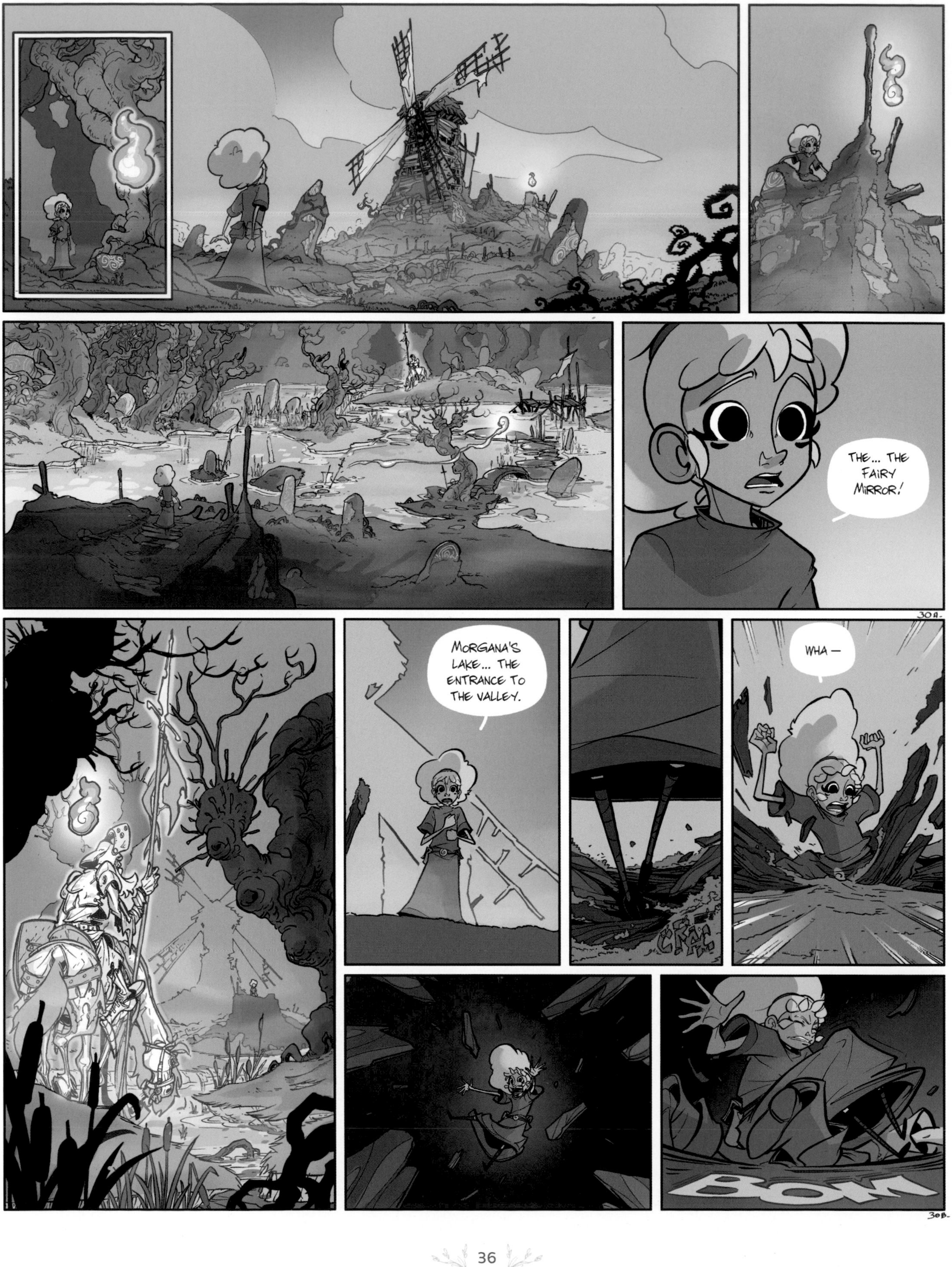
THE... THE FAIRY MIRROR!
30A-
MORGANA'S LAKE... THE ENTRANCE TO THE VALLEY.
CRAC
WHA —
BOM
30B-

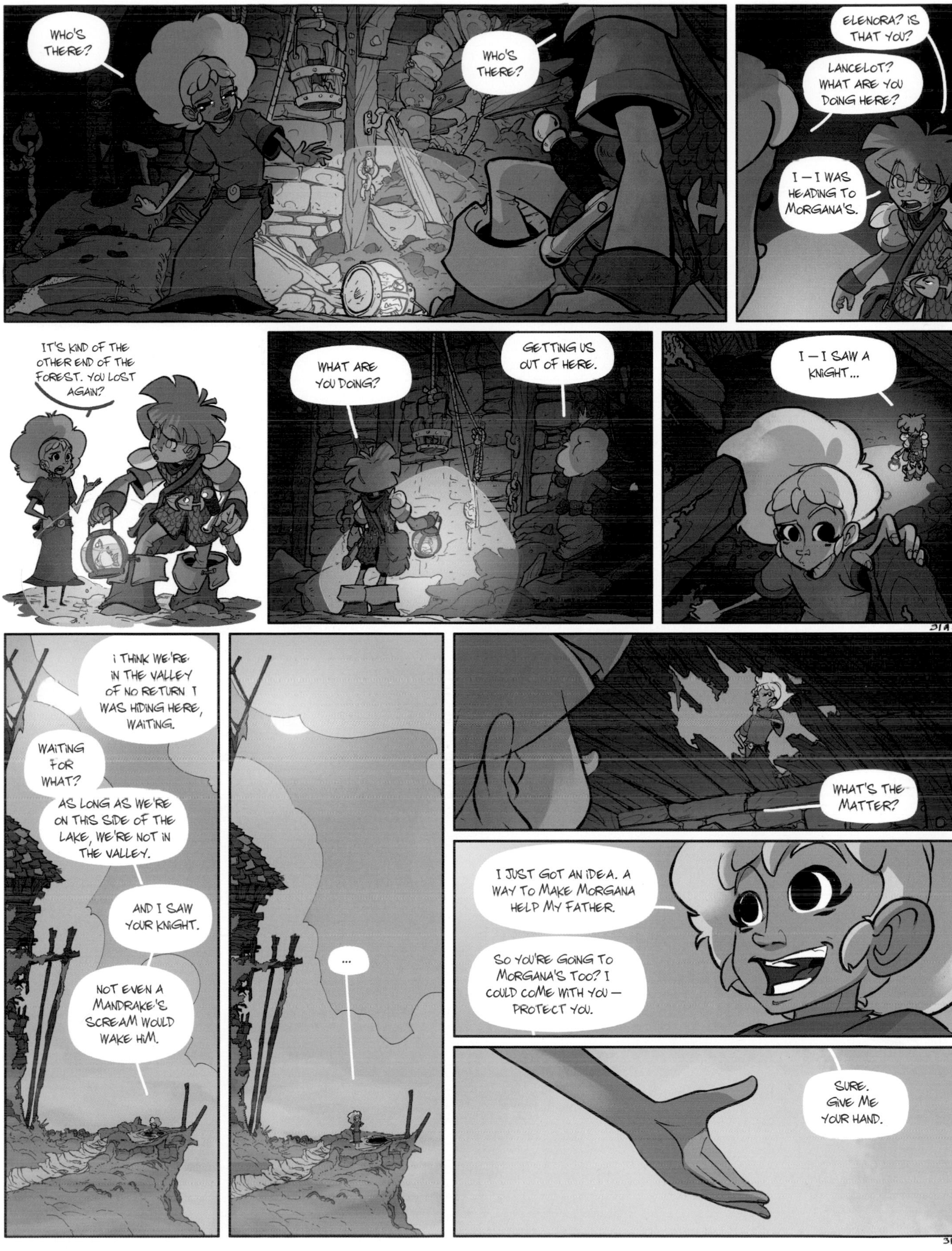
WHO'S THERE?
WHO'S THERE?
ELENORA? IS THAT YOU?
LANCELOT? WHAT ARE YOU DOING HERE?
I — I WAS HEADING TO MORGANA'S.
IT'S KIND OF THE OTHER END OF THE FOREST. YOU LOST AGAIN?
WHAT ARE YOU DOING?
GETTING US OUT OF HERE.
I — I SAW A KNIGHT...
31A-
I THINK WE'RE IN THE VALLEY OF NO RETURN. I WAS HIDING HERE, WAITING.
WAITING FOR WHAT?
AS LONG AS WE'RE ON THIS SIDE OF THE LAKE, WE'RE NOT IN THE VALLEY.
AND I SAW YOUR KNIGHT.
NOT EVEN A MANDRAKE'S SCREAM WOULD WAKE HIM.
...
WHAT'S THE MATTER?
I JUST GOT AN IDEA. A WAY TO MAKE MORGANA HELP MY FATHER.
SO YOU'RE GOING TO MORGANA'S TOO? I COULD COME WITH YOU — PROTECT YOU.
SURE. GIVE ME YOUR HAND.
31B-

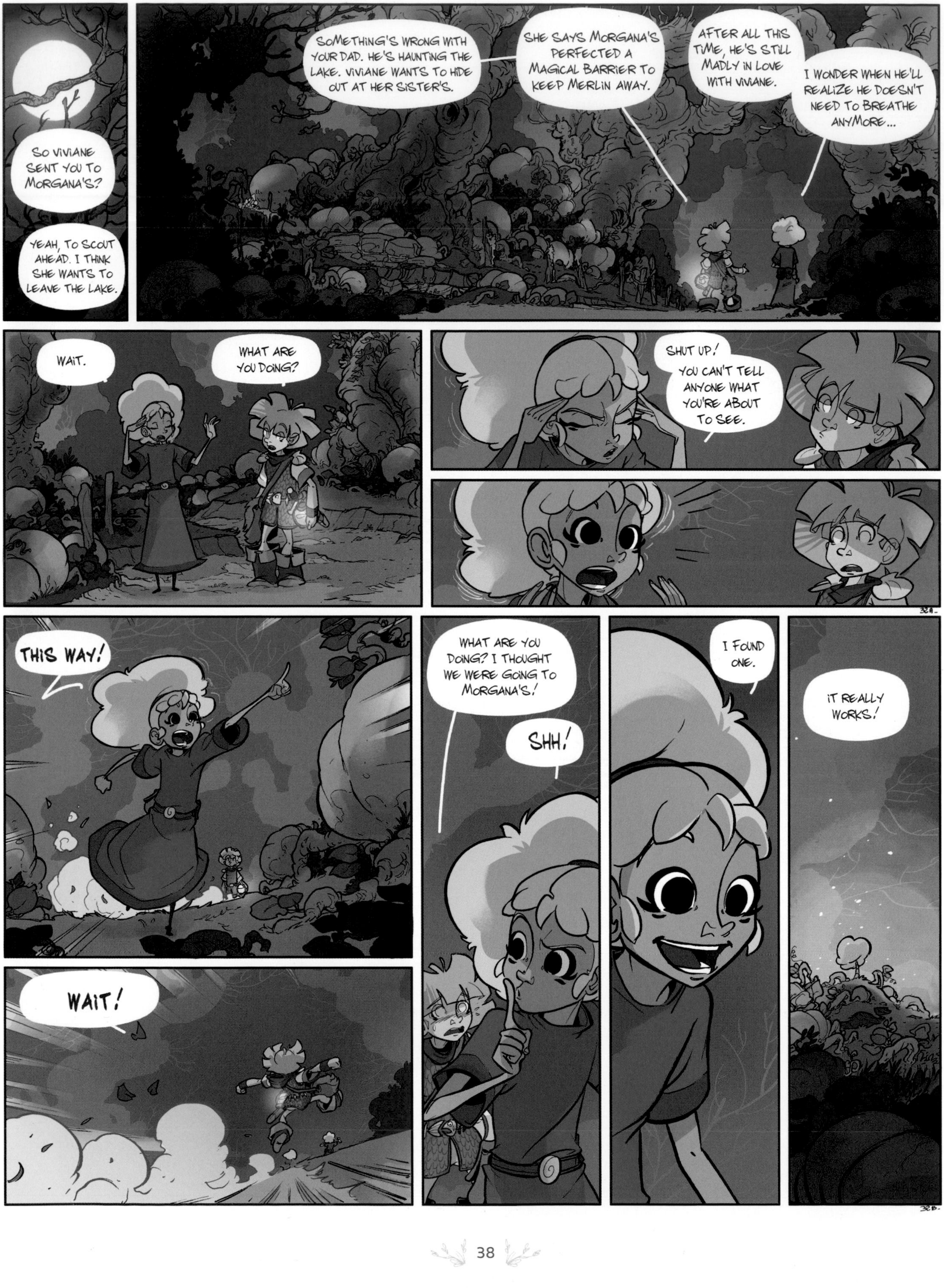
SO VIVIANE SENT YOU TO MORGANA'S?
YEAH, TO SCOUT AHEAD. I THINK SHE WANTS TO LEAVE THE LAKE.
SOMETHING'S WRONG WITH YOUR DAD. HE'S HAUNTING THE LAKE. VIVIANE WANTS TO HIDE OUT AT HER SISTER'S.
SHE SAYS MORGANA'S PERFECTED A MAGICAL BARRIER TO KEEP MERLIN AWAY.
AFTER ALL THIS TIME, HE'S STILL MADLY IN LOVE WITH VIVIANE.
I WONDER WHEN HE'LL REALIZE HE DOESN'T NEED TO BREATHE ANYMORE...
WAIT.
WHAT ARE YOU DOING?
SHUT UP!
YOU CAN'T TELL ANYONE WHAT YOU'RE ABOUT TO SEE.
THIS WAY!
WAIT!
WHAT ARE YOU DOING? I THOUGHT WE WERE GOING TO MORGANA'S!
SHH!
I FOUND ONE.
IT REALLY WORKS!

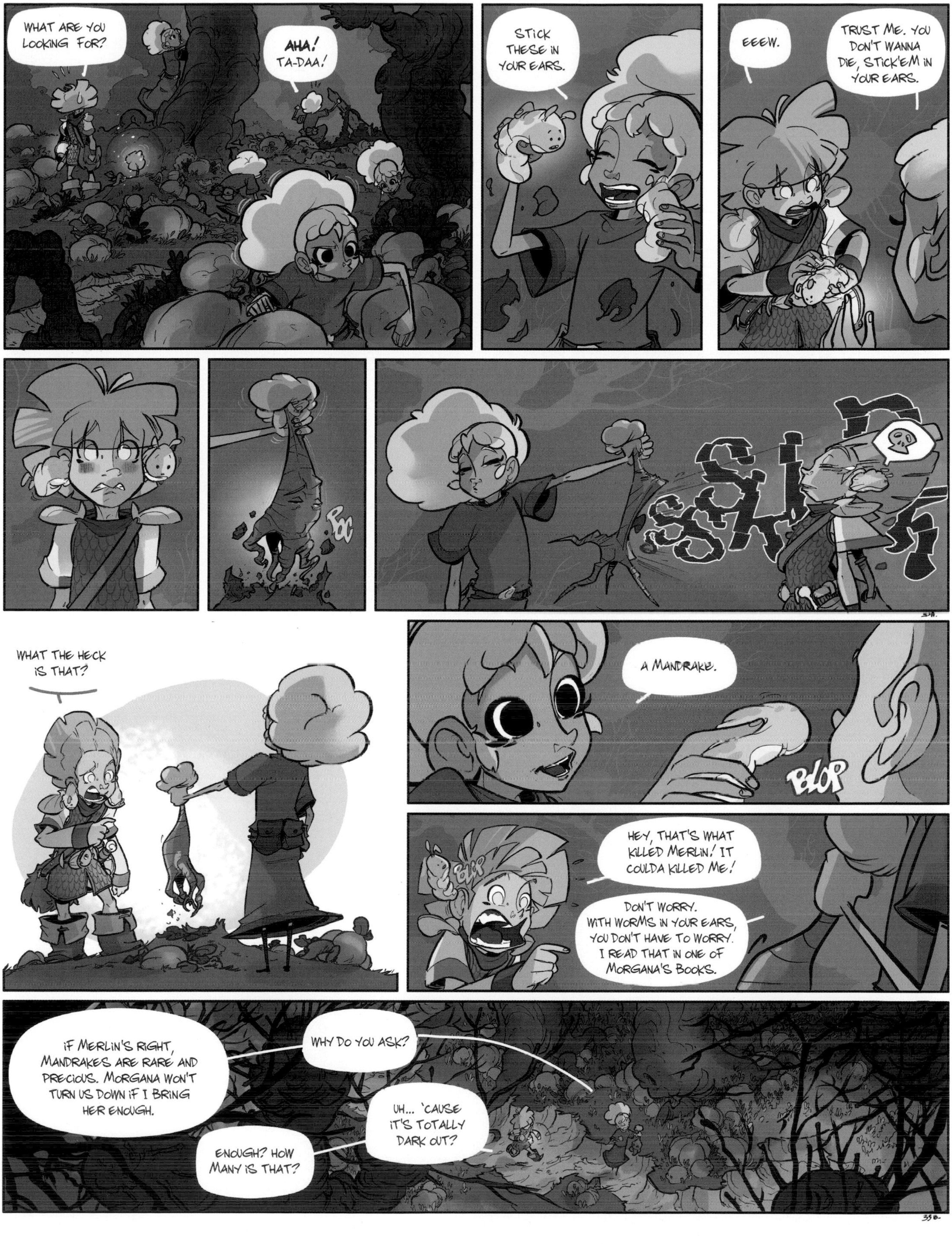
WHAT ARE YOU LOOKING FOR?
AHA! TA-DAA!
STICK THESE IN YOUR EARS.
EEEW.
TRUST ME. YOU DON'T WANNA DIE, STICK'EM IN YOUR EARS.
POC
WHAT THE HECK IS THAT?
A MANDRAKE.
BLOP
HEY, THAT'S WHAT KILLED MERLIN! IT COULDA KILLED ME!
DON'T WORRY. WITH WORMS IN YOUR EARS, YOU DON'T HAVE TO WORRY. I READ THAT IN ONE OF MORGANA'S BOOKS.
IF MERLIN'S RIGHT, MANDRAKES ARE RARE AND PRECIOUS. MORGANA WON'T TURN US DOWN IF I BRING HER ENOUGH.
WHY DO YOU ASK?
ENOUGH? HOW MANY IS THAT?
UH... 'CAUSE IT'S TOTALLY DARK OUT?

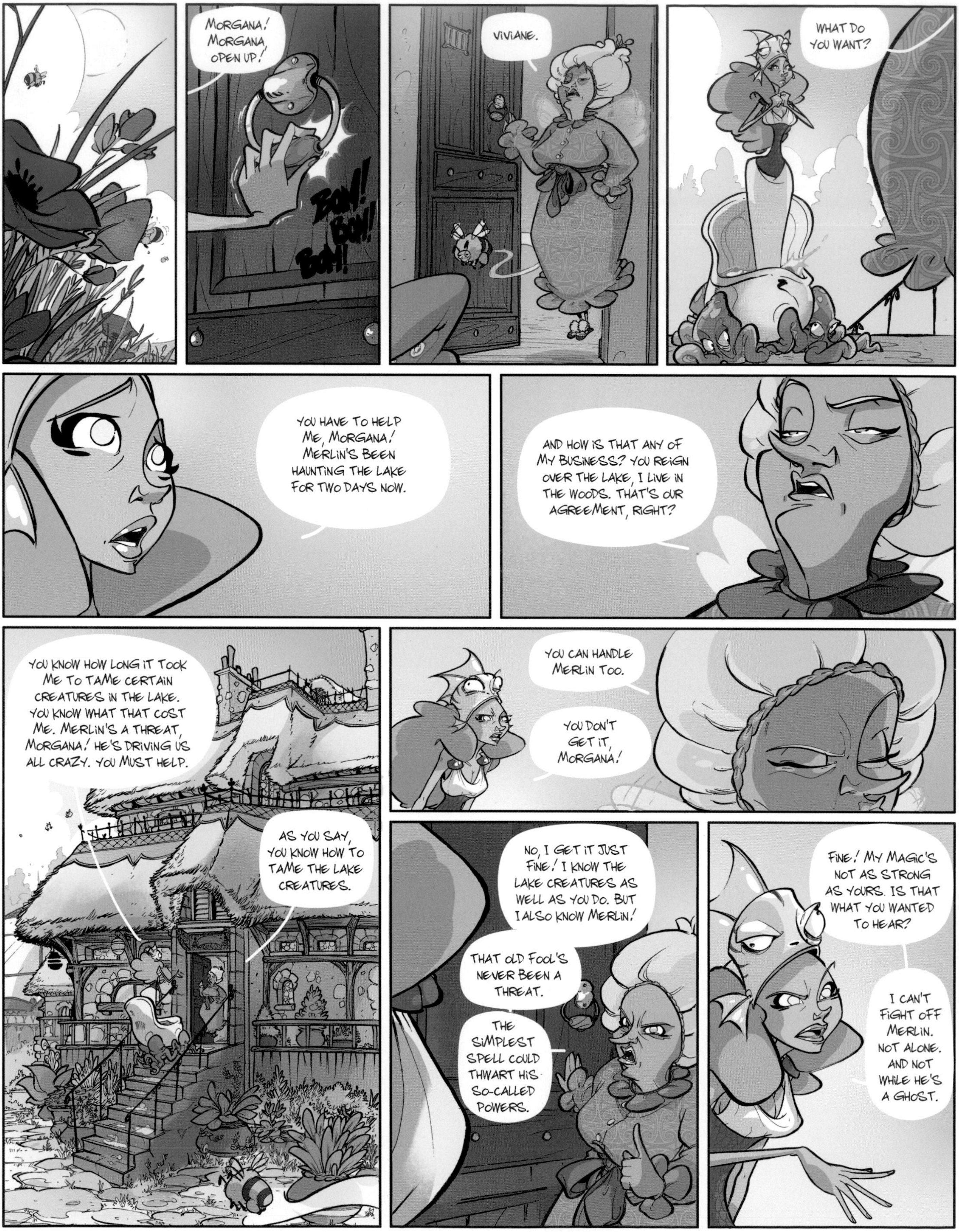

MORGANA! MORGANA, OPEN UP!
BOM! BOM! BOM!
VIVIANE.
WHAT DO YOU WANT?
YOU HAVE TO HELP ME, MORGANA! MERLIN'S BEEN HAUNTING THE LAKE FOR TWO DAYS NOW.
AND HOW IS THAT ANY OF MY BUSINESS? YOU REIGN OVER THE LAKE, I LIVE IN THE WOODS. THAT'S OUR AGREEMENT, RIGHT?
YOU KNOW HOW LONG IT TOOK ME TO TAME CERTAIN CREATURES IN THE LAKE. YOU KNOW WHAT THAT COST ME. MERLIN'S A THREAT, MORGANA! HE'S DRIVING US ALL CRAZY. YOU MUST HELP.
AS YOU SAY, YOU KNOW HOW TO TAME THE LAKE CREATURES.
YOU CAN HANDLE MERLIN TOO.
YOU DON'T GET IT, MORGANA!
NO, I GET IT JUST FINE! I KNOW THE LAKE CREATURES AS WELL AS YOU DO. BUT I ALSO KNOW MERLIN!
THAT OLD FOOL'S NEVER BEEN A THREAT.
THE SIMPLEST SPELL COULD THWART HIS SO-CALLED POWERS.
FINE! MY MAGIC'S NOT AS STRONG AS YOURS. IS THAT WHAT YOU WANTED TO HEAR?
I CAN'T FIGHT OFF MERLIN. NOT ALONE. AND NOT WHILE HE'S A GHOST.

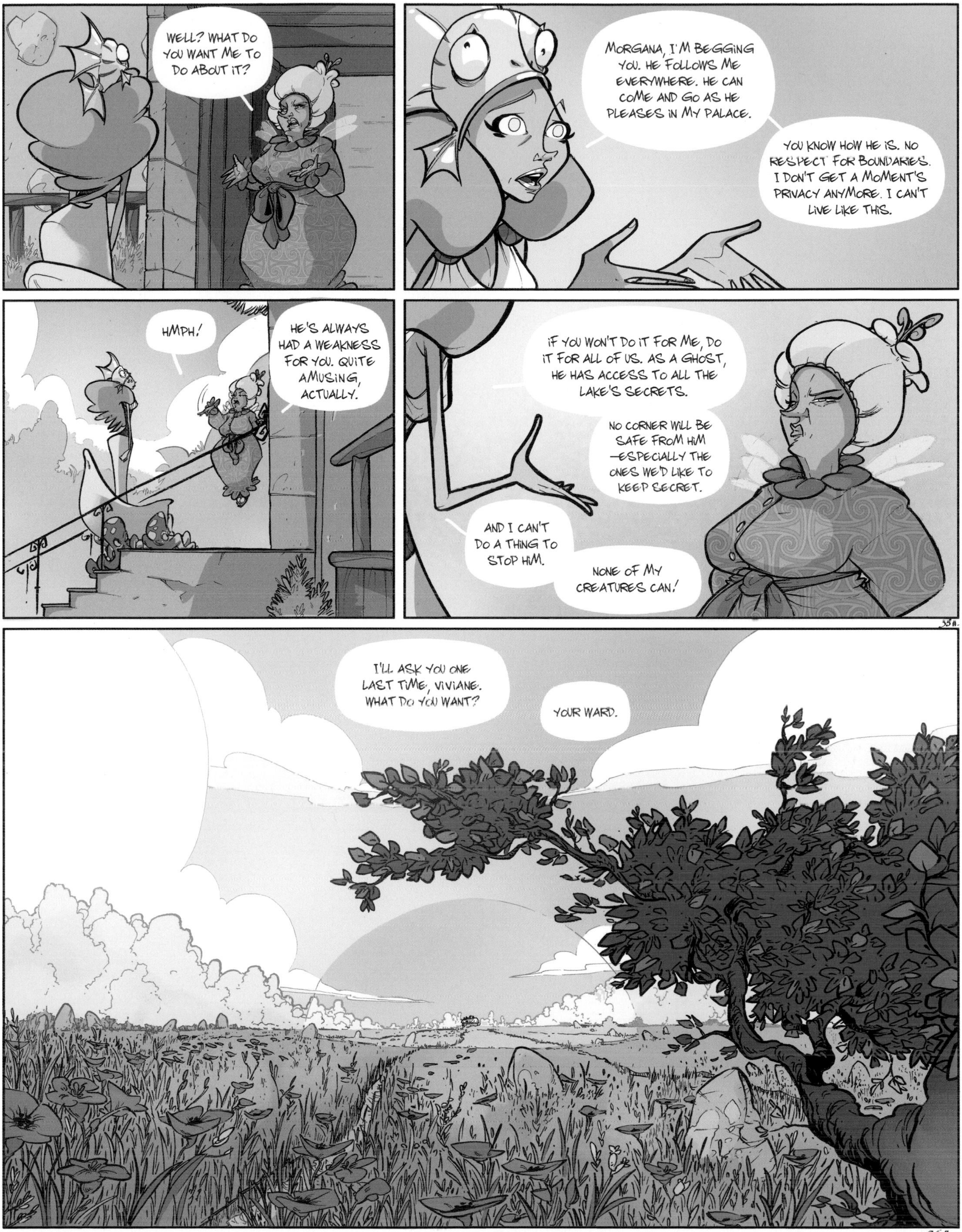
WELL? WHAT DO YOU WANT ME TO DO ABOUT IT?
MORGANA, I'M BEGGING YOU. HE FOLLOWS ME EVERYWHERE. HE CAN COME AND GO AS HE PLEASES IN MY PALACE.
YOU KNOW HOW HE IS. NO RESPECT FOR BOUNDARIES. I DON'T GET A MOMENT'S PRIVACY ANYMORE. I CAN'T LIVE LIKE THIS.
HMPH!
HE'S ALWAYS HAD A WEAKNESS FOR YOU. QUITE AMUSING, ACTUALLY.
IF YOU WON'T DO IT FOR ME, DO IT FOR ALL OF US. AS A GHOST, HE HAS ACCESS TO ALL THE LAKE'S SECRETS.
NO CORNER WILL BE SAFE FROM HIM —ESPECIALLY THE ONES WE'D LIKE TO KEEP SECRET.
AND I CAN'T DO A THING TO STOP HIM.
NONE OF MY CREATURES CAN!
I'LL ASK YOU ONE LAST TIME, VIVIANE. WHAT DO YOU WANT?
YOUR WARD.

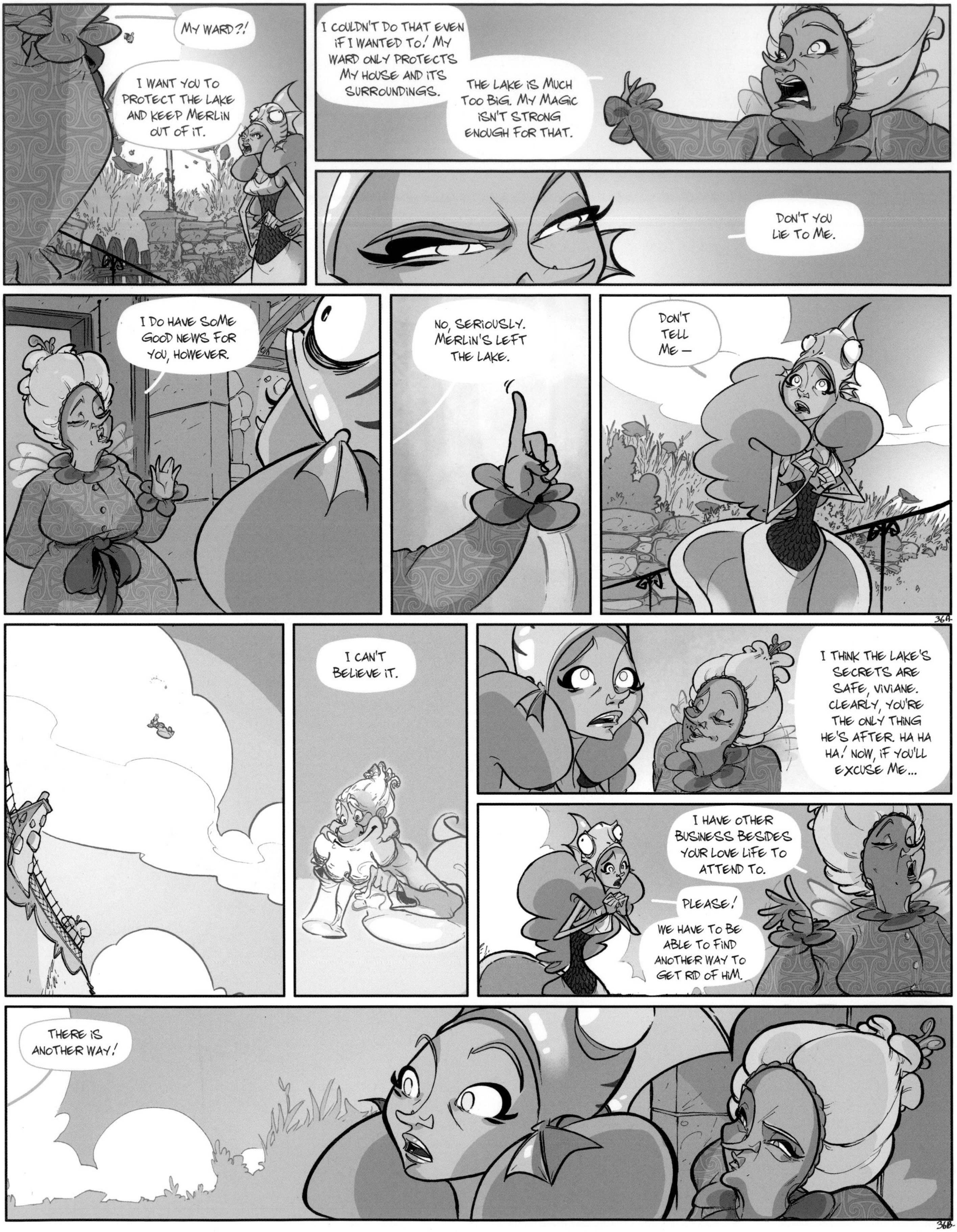
MY WARD?!
I WANT YOU TO PROTECT THE LAKE AND KEEP MERLIN OUT OF IT.
I COULDN'T DO THAT EVEN IF I WANTED TO! MY WARD ONLY PROTECTS MY HOUSE AND ITS SURROUNDINGS.
THE LAKE IS MUCH TOO BIG. MY MAGIC ISN'T STRONG ENOUGH FOR THAT.
DON'T YOU LIE TO ME.
I DO HAVE SOME GOOD NEWS FOR YOU, HOWEVER.
NO, SERIOUSLY. MERLIN'S LEFT THE LAKE.
DON'T TELL ME —
I CAN'T BELIEVE IT.
I THINK THE LAKE'S SECRETS ARE SAFE, VIVIANE. CLEARLY, YOU'RE THE ONLY THING HE'S AFTER. HA HA HA! NOW, IF YOU'LL EXCUSE ME...
I HAVE OTHER BUSINESS BESIDES YOUR LOVE LIFE TO ATTEND TO.
PLEASE!
WE HAVE TO BE ABLE TO FIND ANOTHER WAY TO GET RID OF HIM.
THERE IS ANOTHER WAY!

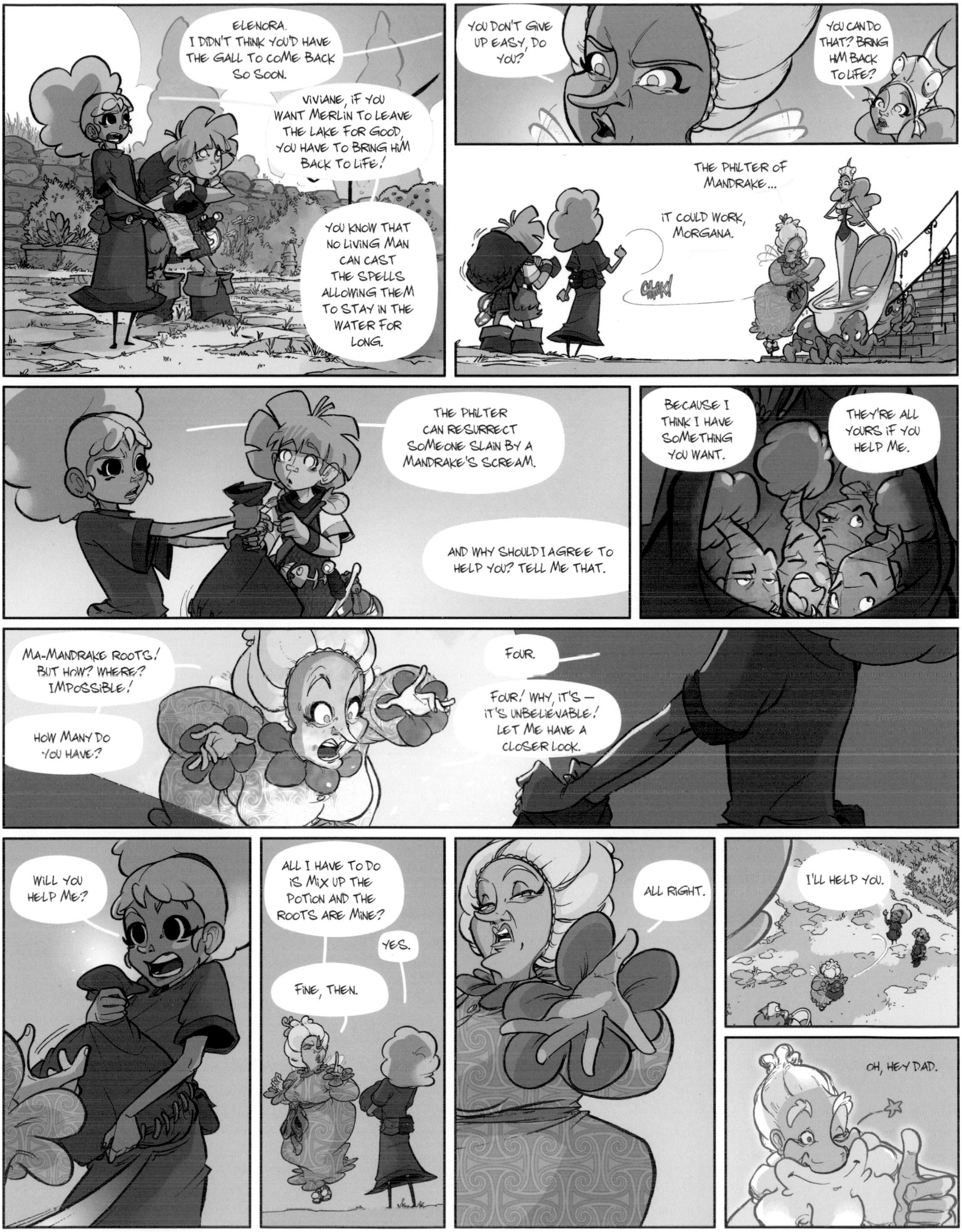
ELENORA. I DIDN'T THINK YOU'D HAVE THE GALL TO COME BACK SO SOON.
VIVIANE, IF YOU WANT MERLIN TO LEAVE THE LAKE FOR GOOD, YOU HAVE TO BRING HIM BACK TO LIFE!
YOU KNOW THAT NO LIVING MAN CAN CAST THE SPELLS ALLOWING THEM TO STAY IN THE WATER FOR LONG.
YOU DON'T GIVE UP EASY, DO YOU?
YOU CAN DO THAT? BRING HIM BACK TO LIFE?
THE PHILTER OF MANDRAKE...
IT COULD WORK, MORGANA.
CHAK!
THE PHILTER CAN RESURRECT SOMEONE SLAIN BY A MANDRAKE'S SCREAM.
AND WHY SHOULD I AGREE TO HELP YOU? TELL ME THAT.
BECAUSE I THINK I HAVE SOMETHING YOU WANT.
THEY'RE ALL YOURS IF YOU HELP ME.
MA-MANDRAKE ROOTS! BUT HOW? WHERE? IMPOSSIBLE!
HOW MANY DO YOU HAVE?
FOUR.
FOUR! WHY, IT'S — IT'S UNBELIEVABLE! LET ME HAVE A CLOSER LOOK.
WILL YOU HELP ME?
ALL I HAVE TO DO IS MIX UP THE POTION AND THE ROOTS ARE MINE?
YES.
FINE, THEN.
ALL RIGHT.
I'LL HELP YOU.
OH, HEY DAD.

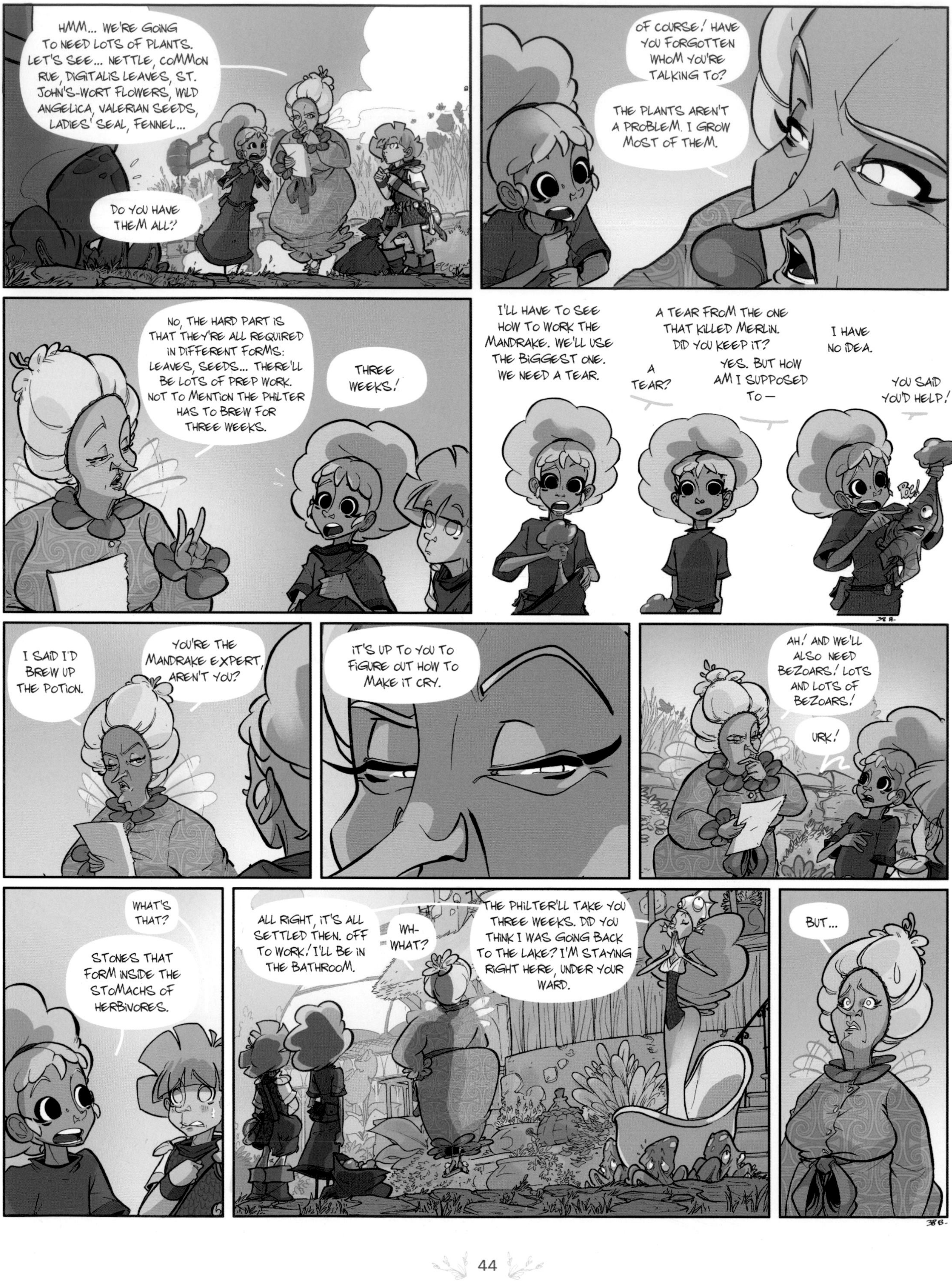
HMM... WE'RE GOING TO NEED LOTS OF PLANTS. LET'S SEE... NETTLE, COMMON RUE, DIGITALIS LEAVES, ST. JOHN'S-WORT FLOWERS, WILD ANGELICA, VALERIAN SEEDS, LADIES' SEAL, FENNEL...
DO YOU HAVE THEM ALL?
OF COURSE! HAVE YOU FORGOTTEN WHOM YOU'RE TALKING TO?
THE PLANTS AREN'T A PROBLEM. I GROW MOST OF THEM.
NO, THE HARD PART IS THAT THEY'RE ALL REQUIRED IN DIFFERENT FORMS: LEAVES, SEEDS... THERE'LL BE LOTS OF PREP WORK. NOT TO MENTION THE PHILTER HAS TO BREW FOR THREE WEEKS.
THREE WEEKS!
I'LL HAVE TO SEE HOW TO WORK THE MANDRAKE. WE'LL USE THE BIGGEST ONE. WE NEED A TEAR.
A TEAR?
A TEAR FROM THE ONE THAT KILLED MERLIN. DID YOU KEEP IT?
YES. BUT HOW AM I SUPPOSED TO—
I HAVE NO IDEA.
YOU SAID YOU'D HELP!
I SAID I'D BREW UP THE POTION.
YOU'RE THE MANDRAKE EXPERT, AREN'T YOU?
IT'S UP TO YOU TO FIGURE OUT HOW TO MAKE IT CRY.
AH! AND WE'LL ALSO NEED BEZOARS! LOTS AND LOTS OF BEZOARS!
URK!
WHAT'S THAT?
STONES THAT FORM INSIDE THE STOMACHS OF HERBIVORES.
ALL RIGHT, IT'S ALL SETTLED THEN. OFF TO WORK! I'LL BE IN THE BATHROOM.
WH-WHAT?
THE PHILTER'LL TAKE YOU THREE WEEKS. DID YOU THINK I WAS GOING BACK TO THE LAKE? I'M STAYING RIGHT HERE, UNDER YOUR WARD.
BUT...

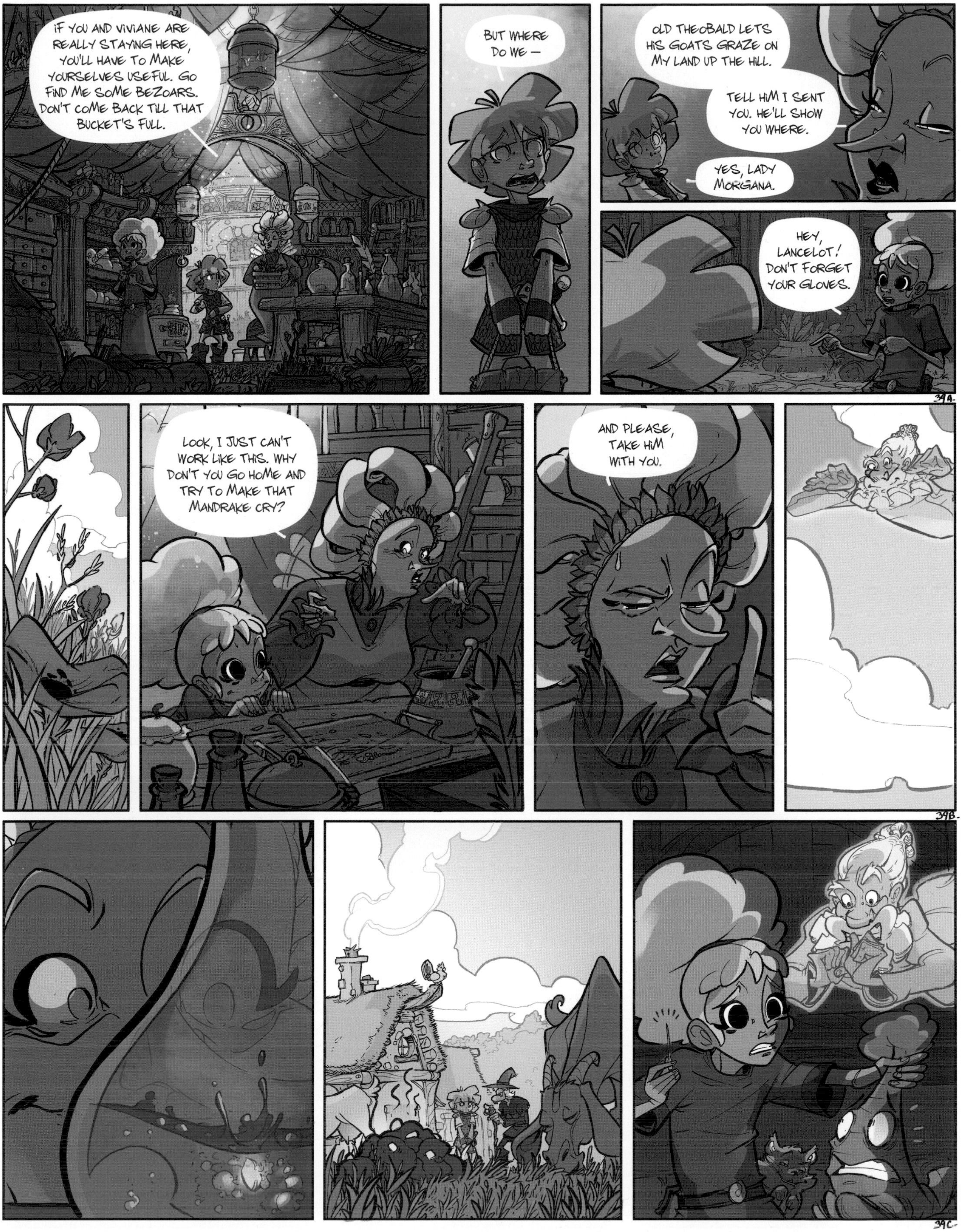
If you and Viviane are really staying here, you'll have to make yourselves useful. Go find me some bezoars. Don't come back till that bucket's full.
But where do we —
Old Theobald lets his goats graze on my land up the hill.
Tell him I sent you. He'll show you where.
Yes, Lady Morgana.
Hey, Lancelot! Don't forget your gloves.
Look, I just can't work like this. Why don't you go home and try to make that mandrake cry?
And please, take him with you.

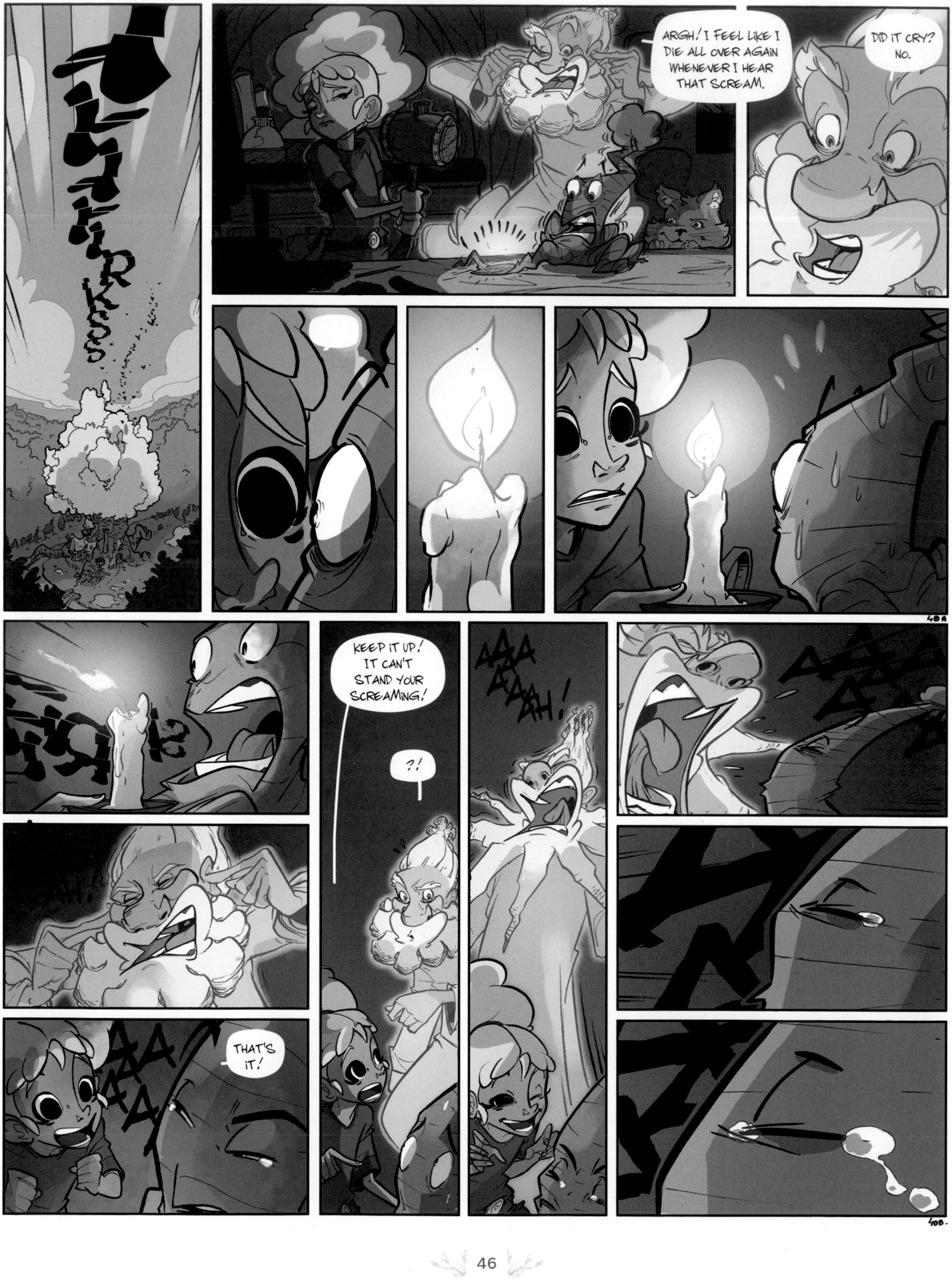
ARGH! I FEEL LIKE I DIE ALL OVER AGAIN WHENEVER I HEAR THAT SCREAM.
DID IT CRY? NO.
KEEP IT UP! IT CAN'T STAND YOUR SCREAMING!
?!
AAAAAAH!
THAT'S IT!

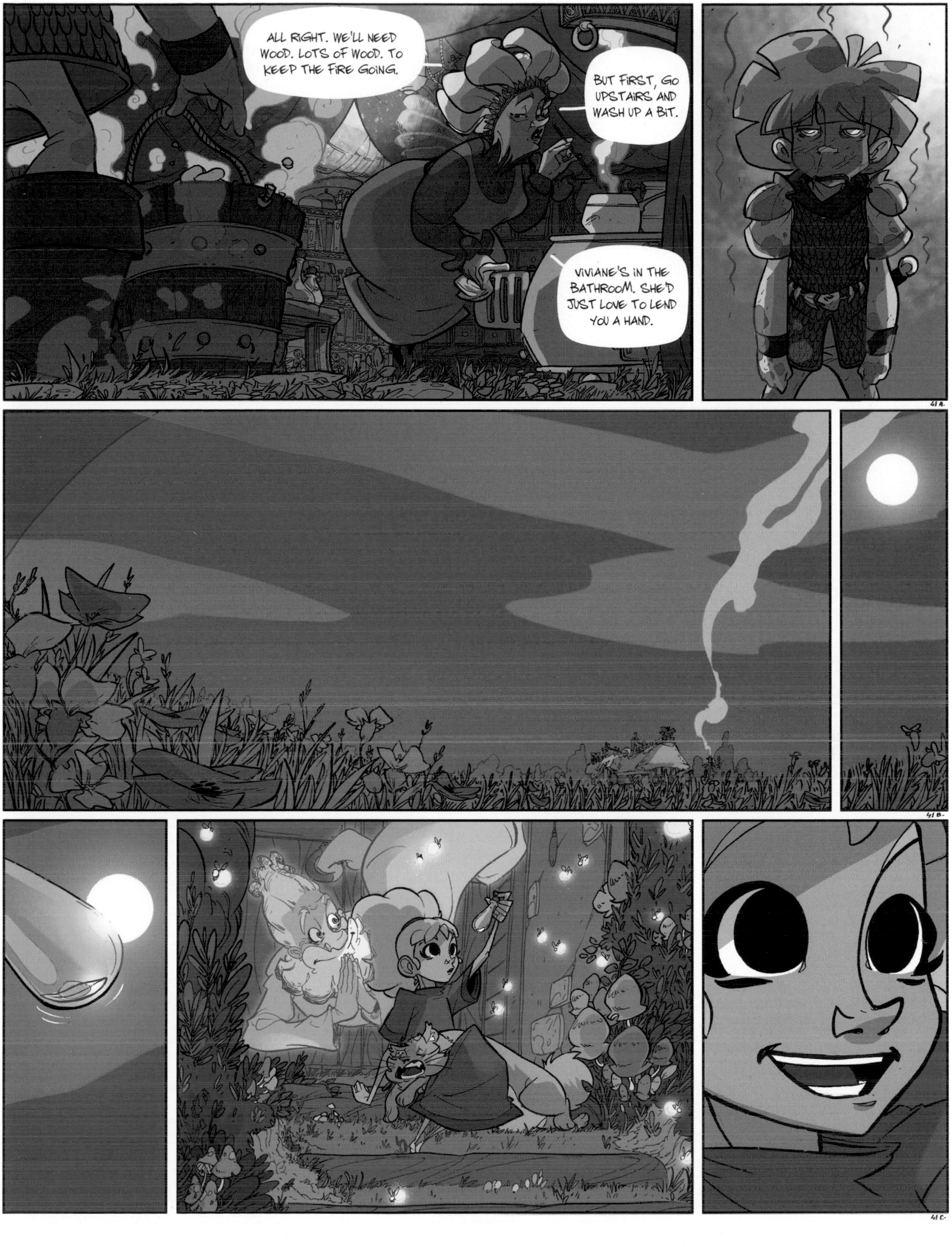
ALL RIGHT. WE'LL NEED WOOD. LOTS OF WOOD. TO KEEP THE FIRE GOING.
BUT FIRST, GO UPSTAIRS AND WASH UP A BIT.
VIVIANE'S IN THE BATHROOM. SHE'D JUST LOVE TO LEND YOU A HAND.

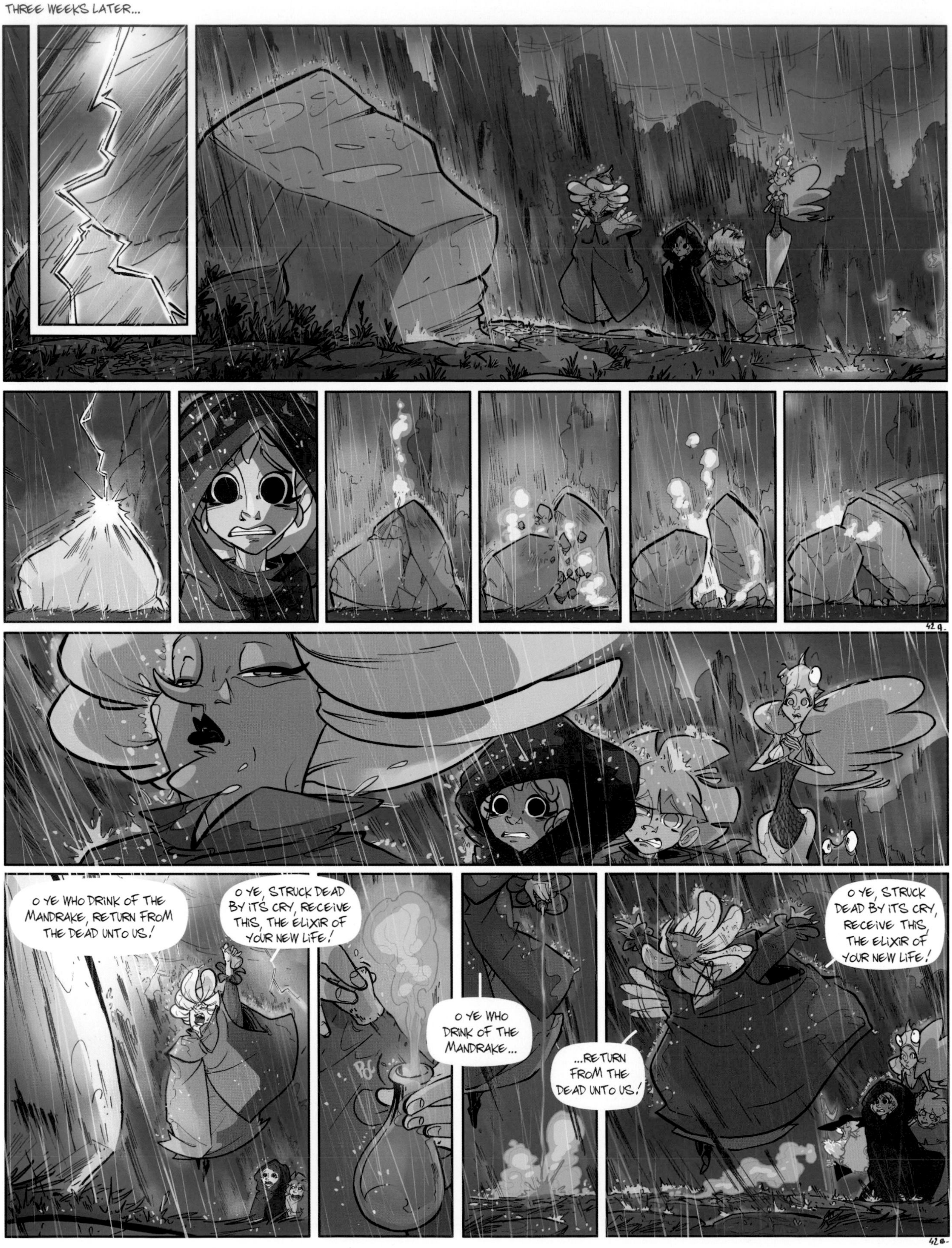
THREE WEEKS LATER...
O YE WHO DRINK OF THE MANDRAKE, RETURN FROM THE DEAD UNTO US!
O YE, STRUCK DEAD BY ITS CRY, RECEIVE THIS, THE ELIXIR OF YOUR NEW LIFE!
O YE WHO DRINK OF THE MANDRAKE...
...RETURN FROM THE DEAD UNTO US!
O YE, STRUCK DEAD BY ITS CRY, RECEIVE THIS, THE ELIXIR OF YOUR NEW LIFE!

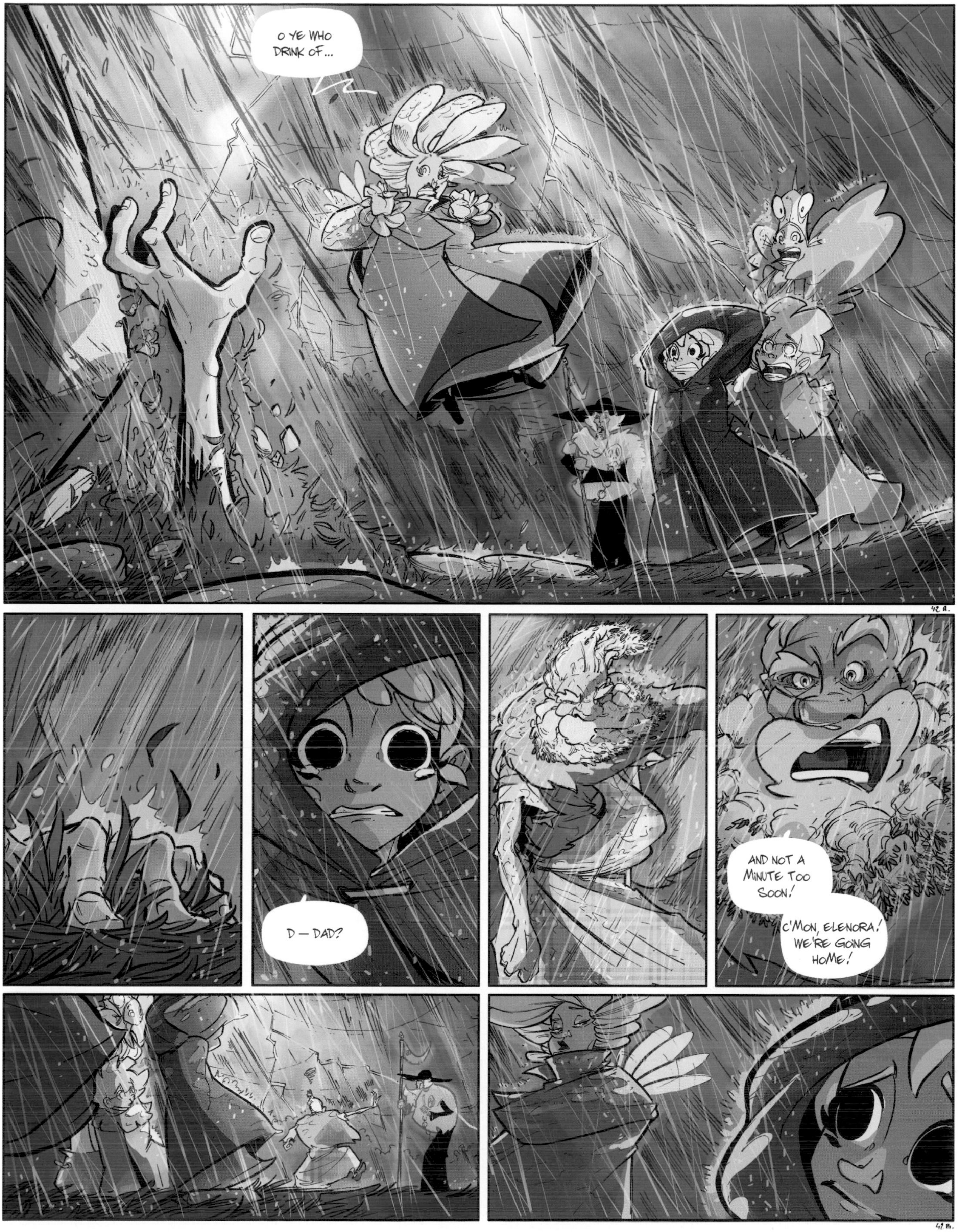
O YE WHO DRINK OF...
D — DAD?
AND NOT A MINUTE TOO SOON!
C'MON, ELENORA! WE'RE GOING HOME!

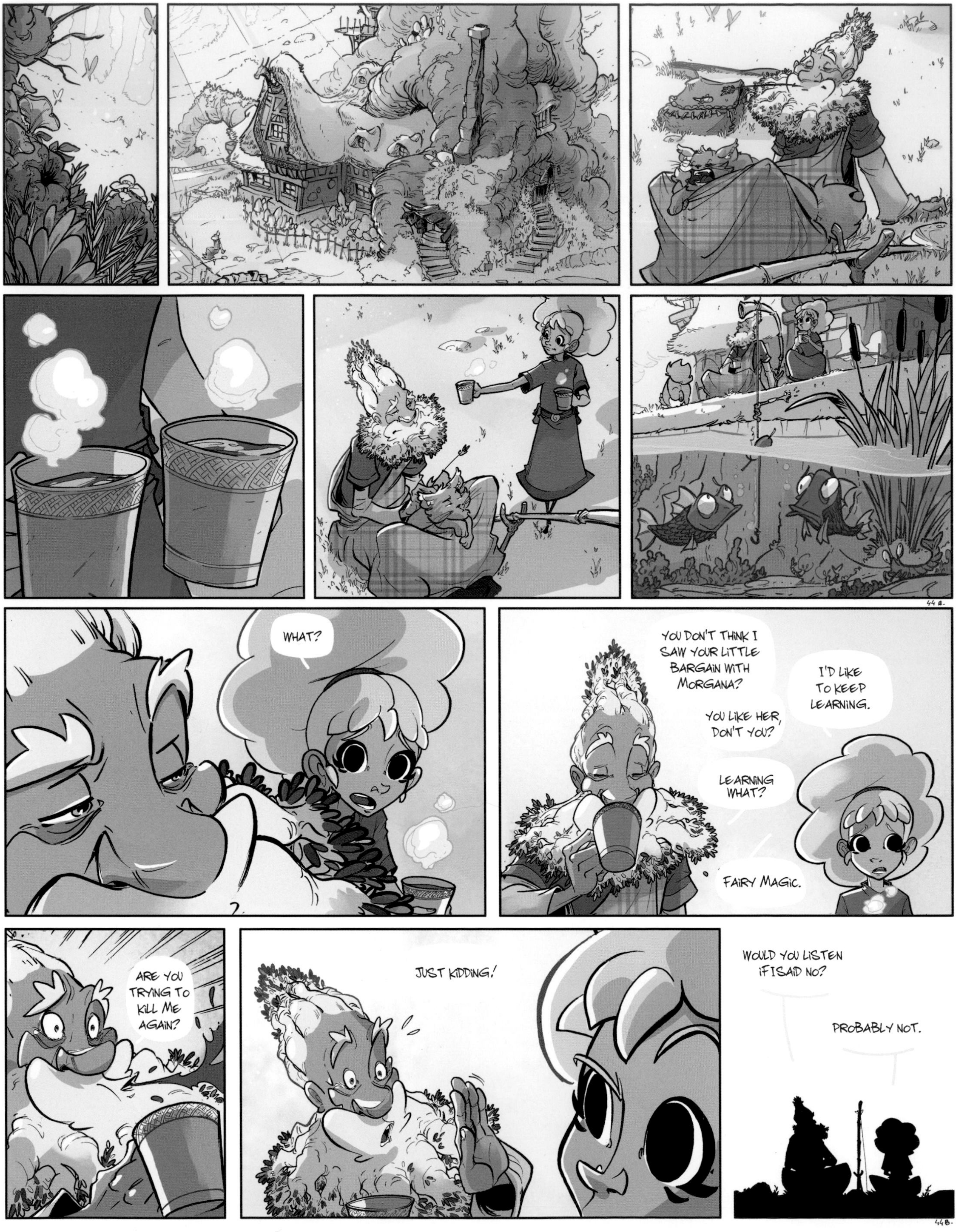
WHAT?
YOU DON'T THINK I SAW YOUR LITTLE BARGAIN WITH MORGANA?
YOU LIKE HER, DON'T YOU?
I'D LIKE TO KEEP LEARNING.
LEARNING WHAT?
FAIRY MAGIC.
ARE YOU TRYING TO KILL ME AGAIN?
JUST KIDDING!
WOULD YOU LISTEN IF I SAID NO?
PROBABLY NOT.

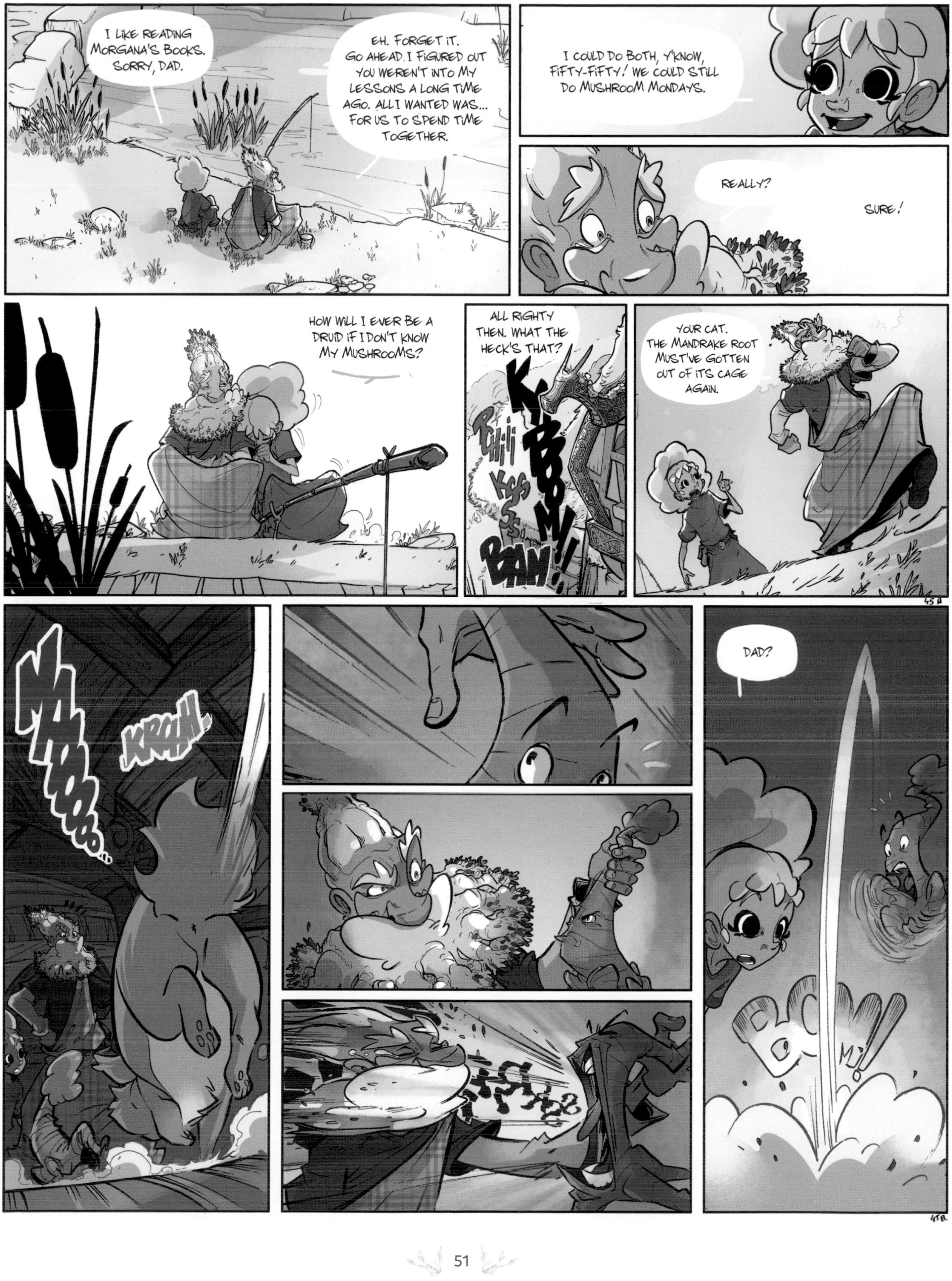

I LIKE READING MORGANA'S BOOKS. SORRY, DAD.
EH. FORGET IT. GO AHEAD. I FIGURED OUT YOU WEREN'T INTO MY LESSONS A LONG TIME AGO. ALL I WANTED WAS... FOR US TO SPEND TIME TOGETHER.
I COULD DO BOTH, Y'KNOW, FIFTY-FIFTY! WE COULD STILL DO MUSHROOM MONDAYS.
REALLY?
SURE!
HOW WILL I EVER BE A DRUID IF I DON'T KNOW MY MUSHROOMS?
ALL RIGHTY THEN. WHAT THE HECK'S THAT?
KABOOM!!
BAM!!
YOUR CAT. THE MANDRAKE ROOT MUST'VE GOTTEN OUT OF ITS CAGE AGAIN.
DAD?
BOOM!!

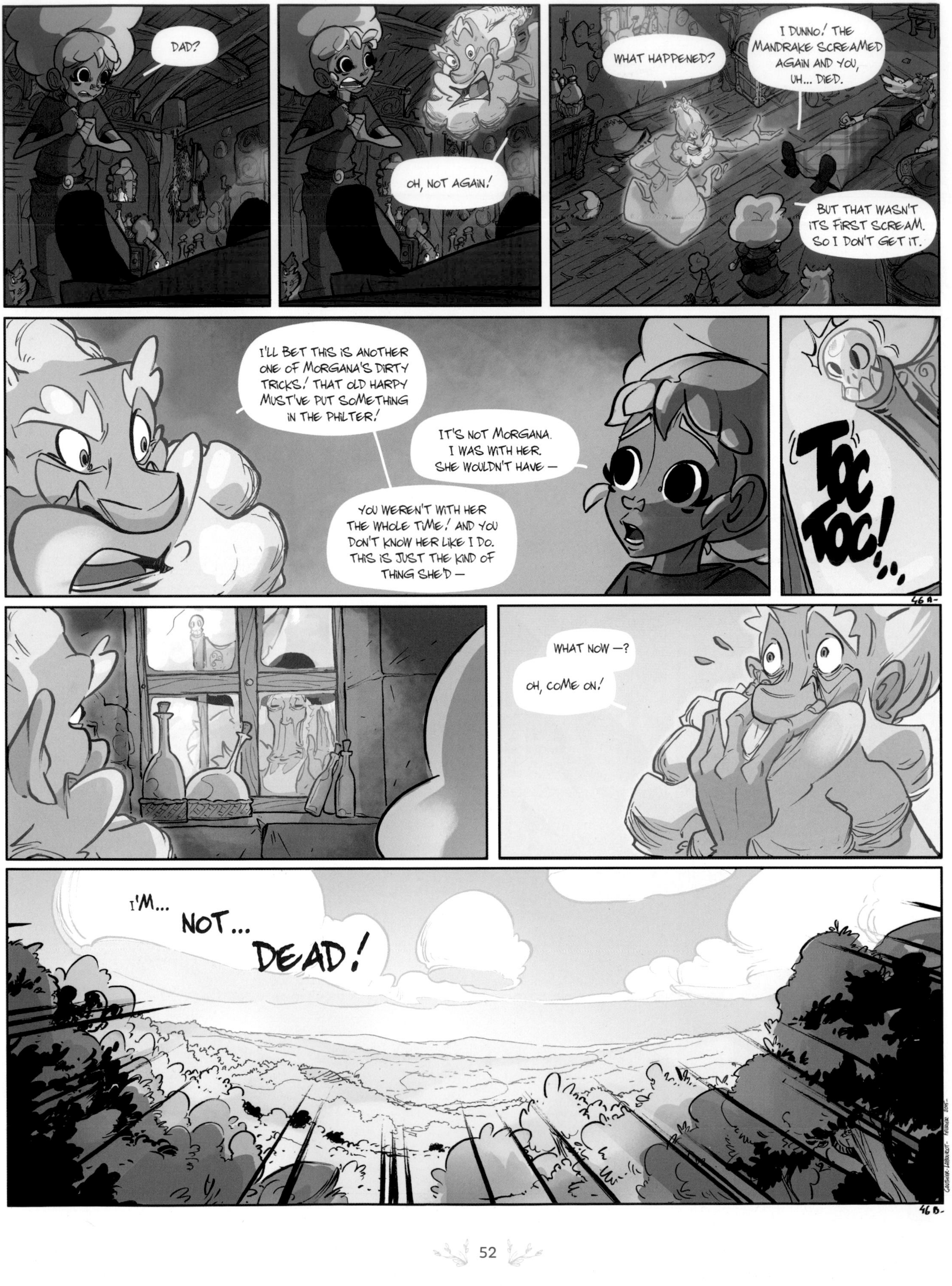
DAD?
OH, NOT AGAIN!
WHAT HAPPENED?
I DUNNO! THE MANDRAKE SCREAMED AGAIN AND YOU, UH... DIED.
BUT THAT WASN'T ITS FIRST SCREAM. SO I DON'T GET IT.
I'LL BET THIS IS ANOTHER ONE OF MORGANA'S DIRTY TRICKS! THAT OLD HARPY MUST'VE PUT SOMETHING IN THE PHILTER!
IT'S NOT MORGANA. I WAS WITH HER. SHE WOULDN'T HAVE —
YOU WEREN'T WITH HER THE WHOLE TIME! AND YOU DON'T KNOW HER LIKE I DO. THIS IS JUST THE KIND OF THING SHE'D —
TOC TOC!
46 A-
WHAT NOW —?
OH, COME ON!
I'M... NOT... DEAD!
46 B-

# The Echo of BROCELIANDE

## Whispers of the Woods

**MERLIN DEAD**
*Morgana Le Fey*
EXCLUSIVE INTERVIEW ON PAGE 2

**EXCLUSIVE!**
*The inauguration of the Great Library:*
YOU'RE INVITED!

**YOUR HANDY GUIDE TO THE FOREST**
*The Valley of No Return*

**POTION PAGES**
*Secrets to a successful Philter of Mandrake*

## Merlin is Dead!

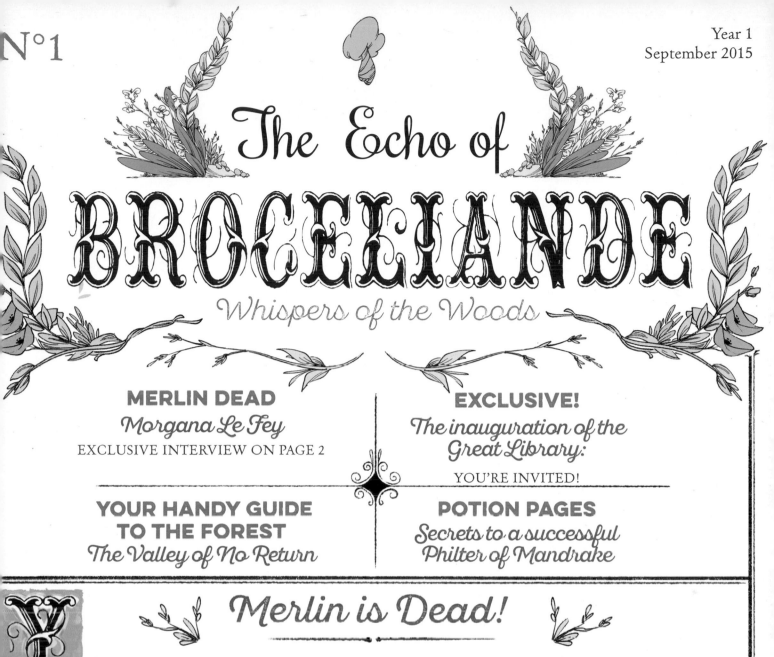

Yesterday, our correspondents in the woods informed us that the greatest druid in the Forest of Broceliande has passed away.

Merlin appears to have died Monday morning under mysterious circumstances, right in the heart of the forest, in the Mushroomery where he spent much of his time studying mushrooms and their curative properties. Merlin's death occurred in the company of the young ELENORA, his daughter and also his student.

Born several centuries ago to the maiden Adhan and a demon from whom he inherited extraordinary abilities, Merlin, master of animals and metamorphoses, was well-loved by the people of Broceliande. He was recognized and respected for his erudition and his formidable powers, but feared for his legendary wrath. Today, the forest people weep for the loss of their greatest druid, while the villagers mourn the passing of a legend. A ceremony honoring Merlin the great will be held in the Broceliande Village Chapel at 11 o'clock druid time, hosted by the fairy Morgana Le Fey, whom some claim has been inconsolable since the tragedy.

# The Death of Merlin
## The Fairy Morgana Pays Tribute

Our special correspondent was able to interview the fairy Morgana in the woods after a moving funeral during which she insisted on paying Merlin one last particularly poignant tribute. Still visibly moved, she kindly agreed to answer a few questions.

*The Echo:* Greetings, Morgana. Thanks for taking the time to speak with us.

*Morgana:* Always a pleasure.

*The Echo:* Can you shed any light on the circumstances surrounding Merlin's death?

*Morgana:* Merlin's death is a tragedy, of course, but it was also a stupid accident.

*The Echo:* You mean it could have been avoided?

*Morgana:* Of course. Merlin was struck dead by the scream of a mandrake root.

*The Echo:* Many of our readers are unfamiliar with mandrakes. Could you tell us a bit more about them?

*Morgana:* Mandrakes are particularly powerful magical plants used in remedies and the most complicated philters imaginable. They also have the potential to be quite dangerous. The act of uprooting a mandrake must be accompanied by specific magical rituals. Without these rituals, the excruciating scream of a mandrake yanked from the soil will kill you on the spot. Merlin, it seems, was careless and only recognized the root for what it was once he'd plucked it up.

*The Echo:* That's surprising.

*Morgana:* Not really, no. Merlin's knowledge of botany has always been limited to mushrooms.

*The Echo:* Rumor has it that Merlin's young daughter ELENORA was on the scene. Can you confirm that?

*Morgana:* Alas, it does indeed seem the poor child herself caused her father's death by pulling up the mandrake root without taking even the most basic precautions.

*The Echo:* Do you know what will become of her?

*Morgana:* Honestly, I have no idea. ELENORA's lived in the woods all her life. Merlin took her magical education in hand, and we all know he wanted her to become a druid. The child has shown a certain aptitude; I've offered to teach her fairy magic. The offer still stands. I don't know if she'll take me up on it. It does seem she's inherited her father's crabbiness.

*The Echo:* Everyone knows that you and Merlin have been enemies forever. Why was it important to you to pay him tribute?

*Morgana:* I won't go into the origins of the longstanding feud between us. Let's just say we failed utterly to see eye to eye on just about everything. That said, Merlin in his day did a great deal not only for the people of the forest, but others as well. He contributed significantly to the Order of Druids; as far as I know, he was the last of their kind.

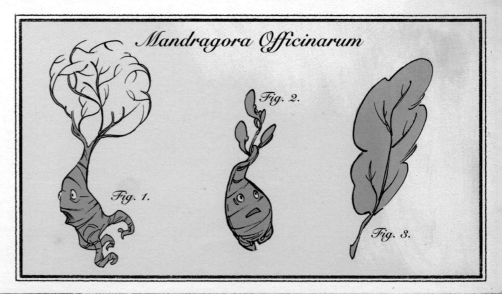

*Mandragora Officinarum*

Fig. 1.

Fig. 2.

Fig. 3.

By paying tribute to him, I wished to acknowledge an antiquated Order that once held a great deal of sway. Please understand, I do believe druidism has had its day, but witnessing the passing of primitive beliefs always brings a tear to one's eye.

*The Echo:* But there are still druids in Broceliande.

*Morgana:* No doubt, but their knowledge is dusty and outdated. Druids are anachronisms, vestiges of a distant past, fossils from an obscurantist era thankfully long behind us. Their influence is nothing like it once was. Their wisdom has been lost. For many years now, Merlin himself had no longer been living up to his own reputation.

*The Echo:* This isn't the first time you've brought up obscurantism. Aren't you afraid you'll scandalize the people of Broceliande Village and the surrounding area, who remain very attached to druid traditions?

*Morgana:* The Order of Druids was founded on a single principle: druids are the sole keepers of knowledge. All learning is passed down orally, and only from druid to druid. The people you mention remain in ignorance, and therefore dependent on the druids. The Order grows ever more powerful as a result.

*The Echo:* You're a fairy, one of the fey. How is your approach to magic and knowledge different?

*Morgana:* In every way! The Order of Fairies is founded on sharing knowledge, making it available to everyone, instead of hiding and obscuring it in mystery and shadow. Fairies are guardians of magic, but we believe in the written word, the power of tomes and scrolls, of education, of enlightening the people. In this way, we are the opposites of the druids. We fairies will allow people to take their own destinies in hand, and in a few years, they'll have forgotten the druids completely.

*The Echo:* Speaking of which, you've announced the grand opening of your library. Can you tell us more about that?

*Morgana:* My Great Library is my life's work. I've been working on it for several decades. It contains the most ancient and valuable manuscripts I've found. The idea is for it to have something for everyone. Merlin's death has only strengthened my convictions: knowledge must be shared, people deserve to know. That's what I hope my Library will accomplish. If Merlin had recognized the mandrake, if he'd known the right rituals, he'd still be among us today. In a way, Merlin's death prompted me to spring into action and open its doors to the public.

*The Echo:* Thank you, Morgana.

*Morgana:* You're very welcome.

The Forest of Broceliande

## Morgana's Great Library

### An Enchanting Inauguration

Private Tours

Led by Morgana Le Fay

**Valid For A Single Admission – Plus One**

1546BD

Visitors are hereby notified that admission includes only the public areas of the library. Venturing into private areas is strictly forbidden.

**Please do not lose your ticket.**

An Enchanting Inauguration

Morgana's Great Library

1546BD

Private Tours

Valid For A Single Admission – Plus One

POTION

# Philter Of Mandrake

*Restores to life careless people killed by the scream of a mandrake root*

**Preparation Time:** 22 days
**Difficulty:** Nightmarish.
**Caution!** Full mastery of level 2 spellwork is a prerequisite for successfully brewing this philter.
**Warning:** It is essential to use a tear from the same mandrake root that killed the person to be resurrected. Using a tear from another mandrake will render the philter useless.
**Helpful Tip:** The Philter of Mandrake cannot be used more than once on the same person.

**Ingrédients :**
*2.5 gallons boiling water*
*1.5 gallons bile from the blue frog of Broceliande*
*4 lb. freshly harvested bezoars*
*0.5 lb. Common Nettle leaves (Urtica Dioica)*
*0.5 lb Mugwort leaves (Artemisia vulgaris)*
*1.3 lb Common rue leaves (Ruta graveolens)*
*1 lb Digitalis leaves (Digitalis purpurea)*
*25 Perforate St. John's-wort flowers (Hypericum perforatum)*
*25 Ladies' seal flowers (Bryonia dioica)*
*3.3 lb Wild Angelica seeds (Angelica sylvestris)*
*0.5 lb Mountain Valerian seeds (Valeriana C)*
*2 lb Fennel root (Foeniculum vulgare)*
*1 lb Mandrake root (Mandragora officinarum)*
*1 tear from a mature mandrake root*

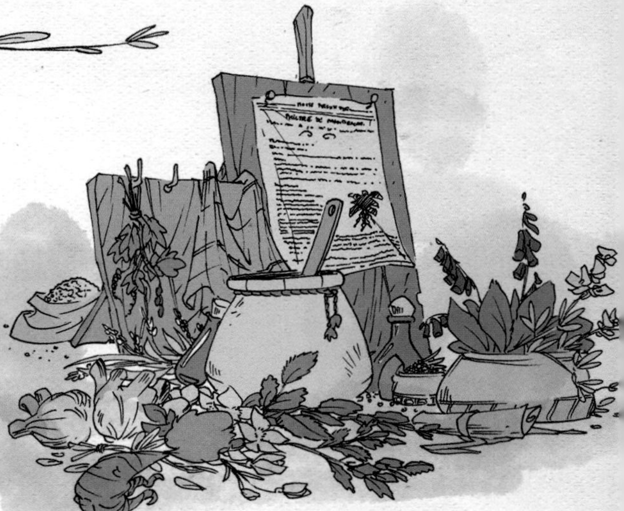

*Fig. 1*

Combine 2.5 gallons of water and 1 gallon of bile from the blue frog of Broceliande. Bring mixture to a boil, and maintain it at a constant temperature of 350° F for the entire duration of the philter process.

Trim the nettle, mugwort, and rue leaves. Let them steep for two days in the mixture of water and bile.

Coarsely dice the mandrake root. Note: the mandrake must first be put under a spell (see petrification spells, level 2, page 325).

Allow the mandrake chunks to soak for 3 days with the nettle, mugwort, and rue leaves in the mixture of water and bile, stirring gently for 15 minutes every two hours. Start by stirring clockwise, alternating directions thereafter.

Add the chopped digitalis leaves at the rate of 0.4 ounces every 30 minutes.

Toss in 7 ounces of bezoars once a day, at the same time every day.

Grind up the wild Angelica seeds. Add the remaining half-gallon of blue frog bile. Stir until it becomes a dough of smooth, even consistency. Slice the dough into 3.5 ounces pieces. Roll these pieces in nettle leaves. Add one leaf per day to the dough, at exactly 10:30AM if the sun is out, or 2:30PM if the weather is cloudy or rainy.

Coarsely chop 1 kilogram of fennel root. Steam it for 2.5 hours, then purée it. Use it to coat 25 flowers of perforated St. John's-wort. Allow these to harden for 5 hours before crushing the flowers and adding them all to the mixture at once.

Once the final stuffed nettle leaf is added to the mixture, bring the temperature of the mixture down to 170°F.

When the mixture has reached this exact temperature, add a tear from the mandrake root.

Allow the mixture to cool to room temperature for twenty-four hours before administering it to the person you are trying to resurrect.

*For more on how to administer various philters and the related spells and formulas, start reading on Page 622 of Phineas Bourne's Moste Potente Potions.*

## YOUR HANDY GUIDE TO THE FOREST

# The Valley of No Return

*Located in the darkest depths of Broceliande, the Valley of No Return remains one of the most mysterious and least understood places in the Forest.*

### A Place of Legend:

Legend has it that the Valley was created by the fairy Morgana, heartbroken when she came upon her unfaithful lover, Sir Guyamor, in the arms of another woman. Morgana separated the pair and turned them into large rocks, each only a few yards from the other and doomed never to touch again. Unfaithful lovers—men Morgana has cursed—remain prisoners of an invisible wall around the Valley and wander, lost forever, in its endless maze of trails till they waste away and perish. To this day, no one has been able to lift the enchantment.

### Points of Interest:

#### Morgana's Lake

The Valley of No Return begins with Morgana's Lake, also known as the Fairy Mirror. Simply a must-see if you're out for a stroll and aren't afraid of getting too close to the Valley. Morgana's Lake owes its nickname to the fact that its surface is always completely still. The lake is located so deep in the woods that the trees keep the wind from ruffling its surface and disturbing the terrible silence and incredible stillness of the surroundings.

#### The Old Windmill

Located near the lake, the Old Windmill is an ideal spot for a picnic. Caution, however, is advised when exploring the surroundings. The windmill has lain in ruins for decades now, and many accidents have been reported.

#### The Unfaithful Lovers

Live the legend! Discover the petrified lovers, victims of the fearful wrath of the fairy Morgana.

#### The Circle of Viviane

The Circle of Viviane is an imposing megalithic structure consisting of no less than twelve slabs of red schist. According to legend, Viviane, the Lady of the Lake, likes to hang out there.

#### Merlin's Seat

Merlin's Seat, also known as the jagged outcrop, offers a splendid panorama of the Valley of No Return. This eroded promontory is located on the moor overlooking the Valley. Some say that on a clear day, you can glimpse the lost knights wandering the pathways of their invisible prison. A favorite meditation spot for the recently deceased druid, Merlin's Seat is now poised to become a pilgrimage site for the late mage's admirers.

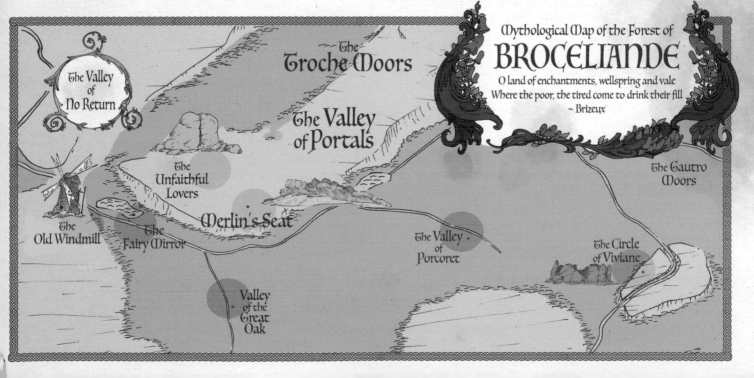

Mythological Map of the Forest of
BROCELIANDE
O land of enchantments, wellspring and vale
Where the poor, the tired come to drink their fill
~ Brizeux
The Valley of No Return
The Troche Moors
The Valley of Portals
The Unfaithful Lovers
Merlin's Seat
The Old Windmill
The Fairy Mirror
The Gautro Moors
The Valley of Porcoret
The Circle of Viviane
Valley of the Great Oak

# SILLI THE DRUID

*Authentic druid*
*Seer – Healer*

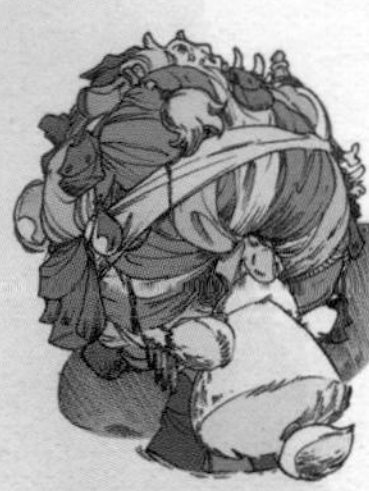

**Heir to deep secrets and powers passed down for ten generations. Healer of maladies, all sorts. Potions and amulets, all sorts, love potions (lover guaranteed to return in under a week), enchantments, disenchantments, communication with the afterlife. Remote viewing by appointment, fortune-telling via runes, coffee grounds, lake mud, spittle, and entrails of the blue frog of Broceliande, telepathy. One-of-a-kind gifts at your service.**

# THE HIVE

*Morgana's honey, nectar of the forest.*

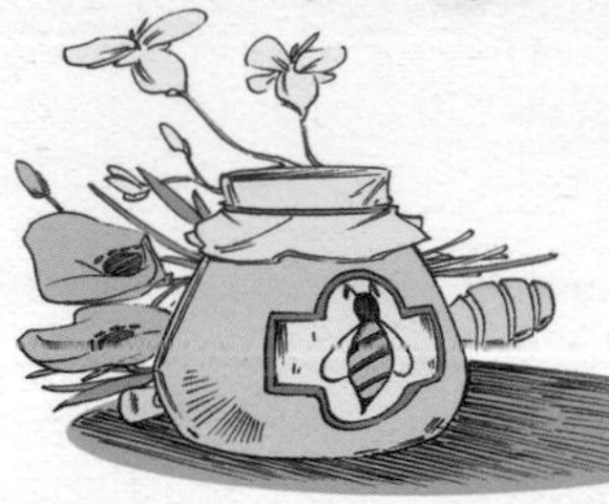

## RUMOR HAS IT

*that the Lady of the Lake has left the Lake! According to gossip, Merlin's ghost is haunting the lake, causing Viviane to seek refuge with her sister, the fairy Morgana. Remember, Merlin and Viviane were lovers once! Is Merlin hoping to rekindle a spark from beyond the grave?*

# LAKE-BOTTOM MUD MASK

*Revitalizing! Energizing!*
*Give your skin that youthful glow again with our unguent made with mud dredged from the very depths of the lake.*

*It really works!*

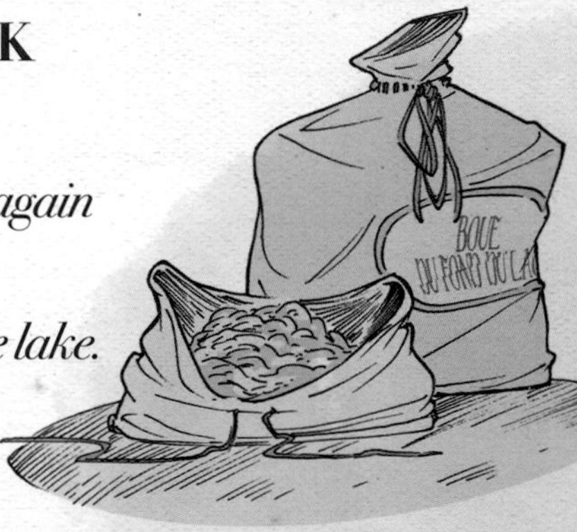
BOUE
DU FOND DU LAC

## HERMIT'S CORNER

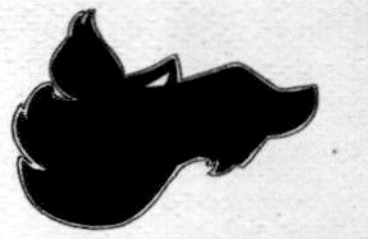

*"Only in times of need do we acknowledge our hermits."*

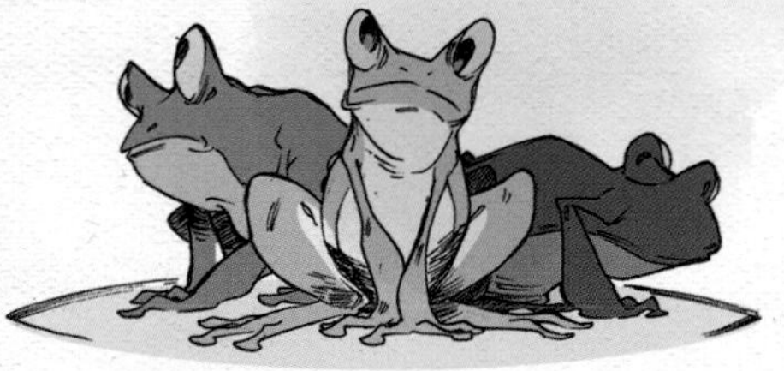

# IN THE NEWS...

Our special correspondents in the forest are reporting a strange migration of Broceliande toads—an unexplained and unprecedented phenomenon. It seems toads are leaving the Great Lake and various ponds and streams, heading for the woods. Our most eminent specialists are on the scene.

## TIPS AND TRICKS

*Better living with plants*

Planting some common houseleeks *(Sempervivum tectorum)* on your roof thatch will ward off thunder and lightning.

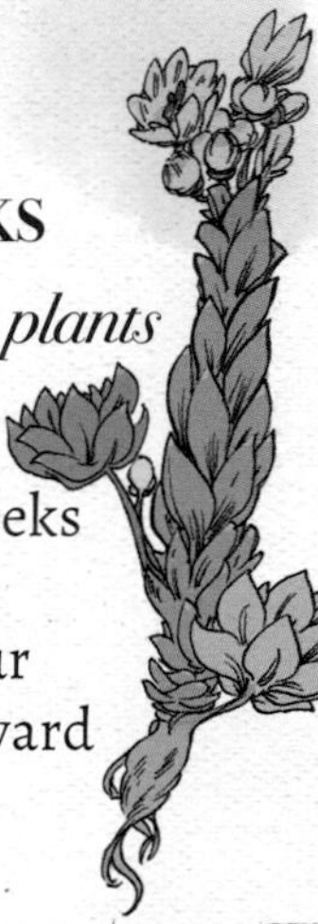

## IN OUR NEXT ISSUE

**Don't miss our exclusive report on blue toad migration in Broceliande, and set out on a terrifying voyage of discovery to the Monts d'Arrée.**

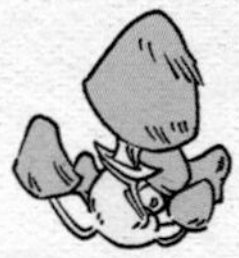

## TIPS AND TRICKS

*Better living with plants*

Pregnant?
A little wild garlic in your pockets *(allium ursinum)* will protect your coming bundle of joy.

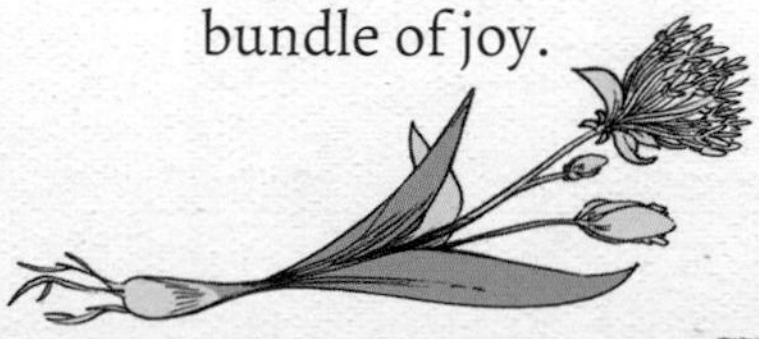

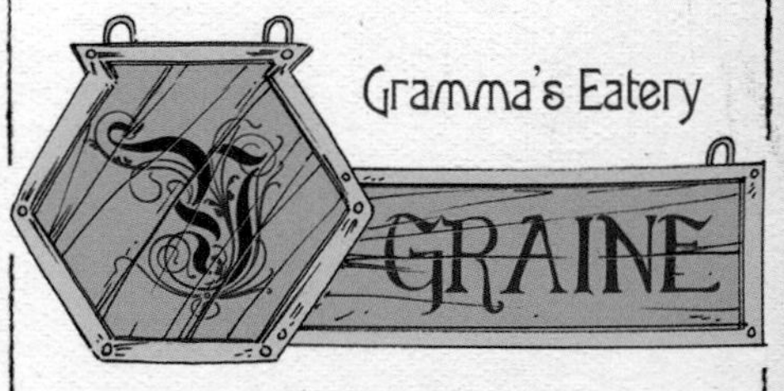
Gramma's Eatery
GRAINE

Roving restaurant in the forest of Broceliande.
Home-cooked, bewitching cuisine
Open 24/7.

# Elenora Mandragora

## Daughter of Merlin